Chloe in India

Chloe in India

Kate Darnton

Delacorte Press

Text copyright © 2014 by Kate Darnton
Jacket art copyright © 2016 by Anna and Elena Balbusso

All rights reserved. Published in the United States by Delacorte Press,
an imprint of Random House Children's Books, a division of
Penguin Random House LLC, New York.

Originally published in paperback by Young Zubaan,
an imprint of Zubaan, New Delhi, India, in 2014.

Delacorte Press is a registered trademark and the colophon is a trademark of
Penguin Random House LLC.

randomhousekids.com

Educators and librarians, for a variety of teaching tools, visit us at
RHTeachersLibrarians.com

Library of Congress Cataloging-in-Publication Data is available upon request.

ISBN 978-0-553-53504-4 (trade) — ISBN 978-0-553-53505-1 (lib. bdg.)
ISBN 978-0-553-53506-8 (ebook)

The text of this book is set in 12.5-point Adobe Garamond.
Interior design by Stephanie Moss

Printed in the United States of America
10 9 8 7 6 5 4 3 2 1
First American Edition

Random House Children's Books supports the First Amendment
and celebrates the right to read.

For Sophie, Charlotte, and Elizabeth

And for Steve

Part One

LOST IN DELHI

Chapter 1

I was so busy I didn't hear Mom come up behind me. I heard her voice before I saw her, and this was what that voice said:

"Chloe, Chloe! Oh no, Chloe!"

I froze in front of the bathroom mirror. In my left hand, I was holding a clump of blond hair away from my head. Well, hair that *used* to be blond. Now it was After Midnight Black.

In my right hand, I was holding an After Midnight Black permanent marker.

"*Now* what have you done?" Mom groaned.

This, I knew, was a rhetorical question—one of those questions grown-ups ask but you're not really supposed to answer.

Besides, it was pretty obvious, no? The evidence was all there: black marker, black hair.

My mom is a watchdog journalist, which does not mean

that she watches dogs and then writes about them. It means she investigates stuff. You'd think she'd be able to figure this one out by herself.

"Why, oh why?" Mom wailed.

Now, *that* was a trickier question. To be honest, I hadn't given the whole thing much thought. It wasn't like I was going to color my whole head with Magic Marker. But *maybe,* if I colored one little section right at the front, then looked in the mirror with my head tilted at *just* the right angle, I could see what I'd look like with all-black hair.

"What were you thinking?" Mom moaned.

Here is what I was thinking:

Every single one of the ninety-eight other kids in Class Five at Premium Academy has black hair. Every single one. In fact, there is only one other girl in the whole school with blond hair, and I've seen that girl sitting alone in the senior school stairwell picking at her split ends. I think she's from Germany, which might be even worse than being from America.

I didn't want other kids to mix me up with the split-end-picking, stairwell-sitting blond girl, so I had decided to rectify—which means fix—the situation.

(For the record, I am eleven, but I like to use big words, mainly because I read a lot. It's one positive side effect of being new and not having any friends.)

Mom had her hands on her hips, eyes all googly. Her lips were clamped into a tight, thin line. It seemed like she was waiting for me to say something.

So I did.

"Well, you're the one who brought us here," I said.

It wasn't me who decided to move our whole family from Boston, Massachusetts, to New Delhi, India, over the summer. My parents decided that. Well, mainly my mom. "It's where the stories are," she had said by way of explanation. I was only ten back then, and I got this picture stuck in my head—the streets of India lined with storybooks. Literally. *Madeline* and *Eloise* and *Pierre* (you know, the boy who says, "I don't care!") were lined up like lampposts along a busy street. Elephants wandered in and out among them. That was what India would be like—elephants and stories everywhere.

Boy, was I wrong. They don't even have a decent public library here. As for elephants, we hardly ever see them. When we do, it's one sad elephant trudging down the hot highway to some fancy kid's birthday party. A mahout sits on its neck, his bony knees tucked tight behind the elephant's ears. He beats the elephant with a stick. Cars and buses honk: Out of the way, you dumb elephant! Out of the way!

Back in Boston, we lived in a tall, narrow brick building attached to other tall, thin brick buildings on both sides. Ours had big windows with black shutters that looked like ears. Huge maple trees lined both sides of our street. The trees were so tall, their leaves met at the top to form a canopy. In the summer, it was like living under a bright green tent.

Our street in Boston was a dead end, so even though we lived smack in the middle of the city, there were hardly any cars and we kids were allowed to play by ourselves out on the stoop. Sometimes we'd sneak white pebbles from the neighbors' Japanese garden and roll them down the steps to see how far they'd make it out into the street. Our building didn't have a yard, but that was okay because there was a city park right around the corner, with a playground and a tennis court and a hill that we would sled down in the winter.

Here in Delhi, we have a park across the street too, but the playground is just a broken seesaw and a metal slide that gets so hot you could fry an egg on it. There's the skeleton of a swing set with chains where the swings should be. The chains dangle there, swaying in the wind. Sometimes street kids tie rags to their ends to make seats, but the rag swings last only a day or two before they fall apart. As for sledding, ha! The ground is flat as a pancake. And it never, ever snows.

The movers showed up at our apartment in Boston on June 13. I remember the date because it was the day after my birthday, the day after I turned eleven. Mom gave them slices of my leftover cake. I watched them through a crack in the french doors. I watched them eat up all that cake, scraping the last bits of fudge frosting from their paper plates with my purple plastic birthday spoons. Then they packed all of our stuff into brown cardboard boxes and loaded the boxes and all of our furniture into a big orange truck and drove the truck to Cape Cod, where they unloaded everything into Nana and Grandpa's basement. Mom and Dad knew we wouldn't be staying in India forever, so they thought renting furniture was a much better financial decision—their words, not mine—than paying to cart it across the ocean. Back at our house, there was nothing left but dust bunnies and seven enormous suitcases. That was part one of moving.

Then we all got on an airplane: Mom and Dad and Anna, who was fourteen, and Lucy, who was a tiny little baby, and me and the seven suitcases. After a very long time, we got off in Delhi. That was part two.

And now a different family lives in our skinny brick building in Boston. A different kid sleeps in my room, while I . . . sleep in India.

Besides moving to India, here are some of the other things that I did not decide:

I did not decide to be a little sister.

I definitely did not decide to *have* a little sister.

I did not decide to go to an Indian school where I would be the only kid (okay, besides the split-end-picking, stairwell-sitting German girl) who is blond. Oh, and American. I am the only kid (besides Anna) who is American.

All of these things just happened to me.

My mom looked at her wristwatch: 7:15. We were going to be late for school. Again.

She let out a loud sigh. "Let's clean you up," she said.

Chapter 2

By the time I got down to the car, Anna was sitting in the backseat, her seat belt fastened, her arms crossed tightly against her chest and her face scrunched up in a scowl. Her uniform was perfectly neat: tan shirt, navy skirt, navy belt, tan socks with navy stripes. There was no mud caked around the soles of her black nylon school shoes. There was no gunk from peeled-off star stickers on her shiny brass belt buckle. A navy elastic held her long, straight brown hair up in a high, tight ponytail. Her new badge—ANNA JONES, UNIFORM MONITOR—was clipped onto her left breast pocket.

Ever since Anna was appointed to uniform patrol, she's been on my case.

"Your socks don't match!"

"Your skirt is too short!"

"Ew, is that dal? Is that *yesterday's lunch* on your shirt?"

Today was no different. "We are all supposed to cooperate when Dad's away on business trips, Chloe. Mom needs our help. Instead, you're making us late!" Anna glared at me. Then she gasped: "What happened to your hair?"

I looked out the window, pretending to see something really interesting instead of the plain old whitewashed wall that surrounds our house.

"We are ready, girls?" Vijay, our family driver, grinned at me in the rearview mirror.

I love Vijay. Even though his entire job is to drive us around all day—a job that Mom says would make her positively cross-eyed crazy—he's always in a good mood. When Mom isn't in the car, he plays bhangra music really loud. Sometimes he sneaks us toffees. And every couple of months, he dyes his hair electric orange with henna.

I nodded. Vijay pressed his palms together in a two-second prayer and then pulled the car out into the street.

"What happened to your hair?" (Anna again.)

I hummed a little before answering. "Oh, this?" I finally said, making my voice all normal-sounding. "It's my new hairstyle. Mom and I decided to give me a trim. I like it."

But here's the truth: I did *not* like it.

To get rid of all the black and then even things out, Mom had to cut off the whole front part of my hair right up by the roots. Just thinking about it reminded me of the cold kitchen shears against my forehead, the ripping sound of my hair being cut. Long, limp blackened strands had fallen to the bathroom floor and curled up there like dead centipedes.

Now my bangs were so short, they stuck up from my

scalp like the bristles of a hairbrush. When I had looked in the mirror, the first thing that crossed my mind was *Porcupine. I look like a porcupine.*

The second was *I look really, really ugly.*

I might have cried a little bit.

Anna giggled. "You look like Lucy."

"I do *not*!"

Lucy is one and a half, and her white scalp shows through short tufts of reddish hair. She is practically bald.

"You do! You look like a baby!"

I crossed my arms over my chest. "Well, Mom says it'll grow out in a month or two, which means I'll be back to normal soon."

"So you don't like it after all," Anna crowed. "You said you like it, but really, you don't."

This is one of the most annoying things about Anna—she's always trying to trip me up, trying to catch me saying something that isn't technically one hundred percent true.

But it isn't the *absolutely* most annoying thing about Anna. The *absolutely* most annoying thing about Anna is that she was born first, and so every year, year after year, she is exactly forty-two months older than me. Anna will always be older, which means that she will always know more things and be better at most things than me.

No matter what I do, I will never catch up to Anna.

As if we weren't late enough, the car got stuck at the red light near school. I know the spot really well because it's the only red light and so all the cars and scooters and auto-rickshaws and bikes and buses—and often a bunch of lost-looking cows—squish up against each other, everybody pushing and shoving to make the turn. There's a small market on one side where the rickshaw drivers double-park, blocking half a lane of traffic as they chew *paan,* pick their noses, and wait for fares. We get stuck there pretty much every morning.

Anna likes to do flash cards on the way to school, but I like to look out the window and watch the world go by. Next to the market there's a small slum built right up to the edge of the road. As the car idled, I watched some men who were squatting in a circle, sipping their morning chai out of tiny plastic cups just like the ones at the dentist's office back in Boston. One guy was cleaning his teeth with a twig. There was a group of teenage boys too, piling carts high with bright green limes, and an old woman with a face like a charred marshmallow, sitting on a charpoy, picking lice from a little girl's hair. When the girl squirmed, the woman slapped her on the side of the head and went back to picking. There were three goats tied up next to them. Then a little kid pulled down his shorts and squatted right next to our car, getting ready to push out a poop. I looked away. Yuck.

Click.

With the flick of a finger, Vijay locked the car doors.

A beggar was winding his way through the cars, coming toward us. He was old and dressed in rags, with a walking stick and no shoes. At first I tried to smile at him, but then he put one hand up on the glass, right in front of my face.

He had stumps instead of fingers. Vijay pulled the car up a few inches.

That was when I saw the girl. She was stumbling across the intersection, carrying a large plastic jug of water in each hand. She wore flip-flops and a pink *lehenga* smudged with dirt. Her shoulders sagged from the weight of the jugs, which bumped against her shins as she walked, splashing water on her skirt. She had to be younger than me. Maybe eight?

As she crossed the intersection, she got so close to our car, I could see the hole in her nostril where a nose ring used to be. The auto-rickshaw next to us inched forward, trying to cut her off. The driver honked and yelled but the girl didn't look up.

When she reached the other side, she ducked down a narrow alleyway into the slum. The pooping boy and the beggar had vanished, so I pressed my face back against the window, trying to follow the girl with my gaze. Where was she going? Why wasn't she at school?

The light turned green.

"I wonder what Anvi will think of your new *favorite* hairstyle," Anna said. Her fingers were still flipping through her flash cards, but her eyes flicked over to me for a second.

Anvi Saxena is the girl I most want to be friends with at Premium Academy. She has long, straight black hair and really long arms and legs. She's like a spider. Not an icky spider but an elegant one. Her uniform is always perfect, like Anna's. But in Anvi's case, it's because all her clothes are brand-new. She once told me she has thirteen uniform skirts and eighteen uniform shirts. To give you some perspective, Anna and I have three of each.

Anvi is popular, which means a lot of people like her, but even I can tell she's pretty spoiled.

There's this long dirt path you have to walk down between the drop-off point on the road and the school gates. Just last week, Anna and I were walking a little way behind Anvi on the path. I called out, but Anvi must not have heard me, because she kept going without turning around. A maid and a man followed a few steps behind her. The maid was tiny, but the man was tall for an Indian, and he wore a dark gray uniform with buttoned loops on the shoulders. When he heard me call Anvi's name, he glanced back. His eyes were hidden by mirrored sunglasses and he wore an earpiece in one ear. He didn't smile or anything, just turned back around and kept following Anvi.

Right before she got to the school gate, Anvi stopped short and held her arms out from her sides. The maid stepped forward. She slid a backpack over Anvi's shoulders and then squatted down to straighten Anvi's skirt and retie her shoelaces. Anvi gave a little flick of her wrist, like she was shooing away a fly, and the maid stood up. Then Anvi stepped through the school gate while the maid and the guy in the uniform turned and headed back down the path toward Anna and me.

"Seriously? You wanna be friends with *that*?" Anna said.

Look, I'll admit it: Anvi is a bit of a princess. But she's also the only kid in my class who spends every summer in

America, so she gets where I'm coming from. And she's the only kid who came up to me on the first day and tried to be friends.

I was standing alone in a corner of the playground, trying to look very interested in the dust circles I was drawing with the tip of my sneaker, when Anvi marched right up to me and told me that her cousins live in Manhattan and that they have fair skin because their mom is a "real" American. She put her hand around my wrist and flipped my arm over so that the underside was exposed. Then she poked at my veins with one finger.

"You can see theirs even better than yours," she said. "They're more green."

"You have nail polish on," I said.

Anvi dropped my wrist. She held her long, thin fingers up in front of her face and waggled them so that her pink nail polish sparkled in the sun.

"Always."

"Is that, um, allowed?"

Anvi shrugged.

"Have you been to Disney World?" she said.

I shook my head.

"Universal Studios?"

I shook my head again.

She frowned for a moment. "Broadway?"

"I saw *Mary Poppins* once?" Something told me I probably shouldn't mention that it was a middle-school production. And that I saw it in the basement of the Boston Public Library with my nana.

Anvi grabbed my hand and pulled me toward the swings. "That'll do," she said.

Vijay was slowing the car down. We were nearing the drop-off point. We had only a few seconds to jump out before the traffic wardens would blow their whistles and wave Vijay on. The black SUV behind us was already honking, trying to get us to hurry up.

I grabbed the door handle. "You're just jealous," I said to Anna. "You want to be friends with Anvi, too."

"Yeah, right—" Anna started to say, but I slipped out of the car and slammed the door before she could finish her sentence—and trip me up again.

Chapter 3

Everything was going okay till art class.

More than okay. Good, everything was good. During morning assembly, they skipped the national anthem, which is when I feel the stupidest because even though I've been at Premium Academy for two whole months already, I can hardly speak a word of Hindi. I just stand there, moving my lips while everybody else sings.

Come to think of it, I don't know why I should be singing the national anthem anyway. It's not *my* national anthem.

After assembly we had free reading time, which I love because I'm a really good reader and Ms. Puri put my name up on the Reading Wall.

Ms. Puri is my class teacher. Compared to the other teachers at Premium Academy, she's a little zany. She wears baggy *salwar kameezes* in bright colors, with patterns like polka dots and chevrons. (*Chevron* is my new favorite word. It's those zigzaggy lines that go up and down like mountain peaks. You can look it up.) Ms. Puri has half a dozen different pairs of glasses, all with thick, candy-colored rims. Sometimes her glasses don't match her outfits and then she throws her hands up in the air and says, "Well, I woke up feeling *gulabi*!" And that whole day she writes on the blackboard with pink chalk and marks our papers in pink ink. It's a little kiddie for Class Five kids, but everybody secretly loves it.

The other teachers at Premium Academy keep their black hair long, but Ms. Puri cuts hers short. Not porcupine short, but golden retriever short. And she's the only female teacher I can think of who's a "Ms." All the others are "Miss" or "Mrs."

After reading, there was math and I got not one but two green check marks—Ms. Puri was wearing green glasses today—for excellent work. Then, instead of Indian breakfast, we got good old American cornflakes, so I took three helpings. And then, during first break, Anvi said I could be an alternate for the dance routine she was choreographing with her best friend, Prisha Kapoor. I got to sit on the steps and take notes.

So you see, it was a pretty good day. I was so busy, I even forgot about my hair.

That is, until art class.

As soon as we stepped into the art room, Mrs. Singh announced that she was breaking us up into pairs.

I crossed my fingers behind my back, but it didn't help.

"Chloe and Dhruv," Mrs. Singh called out.

I groaned.

Mrs. Singh glared down at me. She is tall and skinny and has a nose with a crook in it, like a real live witch.

"Do we have some problem, Chloe?" she asked.

I looked down at the floor. "No, ma'am."

That was not true. I did have a problem. A *big* problem, and its name was Dhruv Gupta, the most annoying boy in all of Class Five. Dhruv's nose is always runny. On my very first day at school, back in July, he danced around me, saying, "Ooh, look at me. My name is Chhole! I am from America!" When I tried to make him stop, I might have sort of pushed him a little. And then he tripped over his *own* feet and fell down and chipped his front tooth on the edge of the slide and Ms. Puri called my mom and when my mom picked me up from school at the end of the day, she said, "Really, Chloe? On day one? Day *one*?"

When I tried to explain that *he* was the one who started it by making fun of my name, Mom actually laughed.

"He was calling me 'chickpea,' Mom. *Chhole* is, like, some kind of cooked chickpea dish."

"Well, I think it's cute." Mom ruffled my hair. "My little garbanzo bean."

Dhruv and I have been enemies ever since.

As soon as Mrs. Singh turned her back to hand the papers out, Dhruv crossed his eyes at me.

How original.

"Our project today is portraits," announced Mrs. Singh. "You have exactly fifteen minutes to draw your partner. No erasers. We start"—she paused for dramatic timing—"now!"

I like drawing dogs and 3-D shapes. I do not like drawing runny-nosed, chipped-tooth boys named Dhruv Gupta. So when Dhruv said he'd go first, I just nodded and sat cross-legged on the floor.

Dhruv sat across from me, his paper on top of a big hardcover book that he balanced on his knees.

There are no tables and chairs in the art room, which I thought was weird at first, but now I'm used to it. In India, people sit on the floor more than they do in America.

For the first three minutes, I sat still, listening to the sound of pencils scraping against paper. The air was heavy and sticky with rain that refused to fall. It was hot. Delhi was having a bad monsoon season. Every morning, when Dad checked the weather, it was the same story: temperature in the high thirties to low forties—that's in the hundreds back home—record humidity, no rain.

The park across the street from our house was drying up. Even though Dechen, our housekeeper, wiped the terrace down every morning, by evening it was coated in a thick layer of dust again. If I licked my finger, I could write my whole name on the glass-topped table.

The heat in Delhi is different from summer heat in Boston, where you know it'll last only a couple of weeks. Besides, you can always throw on a bathing suit and go to the spray park or cool off in the air-conditioned public library for a while. Delhi heat is heavy and wet and there is no escaping it. It's all around you, every day, pushing against your skin, into your lungs. It's like living in a greenhouse with no walls.

At school, it's even worse than at home, where Mom will sometimes click on the air conditioner in her office and let us play cards on the marble floor under the gush of icy air. The school's concrete walls trap the heat and there's no AC except in a few tiny pockets: the principal's office and the sickroom. One time I pretended to have a tummy ache, just so I could lie down on the sister's cool white sheets. After twenty minutes, though, she sent me back to class.

I watched the ceiling fan turn in lazy circles, pushing hot air around the art room. The corners of Dhruv's paper fluttered. I tried to sneak a peek, but he pulled his knees closer to his chest so that I couldn't see.

Out of the corner of my eye, I glanced at the clock. Only five minutes had passed. Sweat was gathering at my hairline. It tickled. If I didn't wipe it soon, the sweat would slide down between my eyebrows and along the side of my nose.

I reached up and wiped my forehead with the back of my hand.

"Ma'am!" Dhruv yelled. "Chhole is fidgeting!"

I gritted my teeth. "I am *not* a chickpea," I hissed. "My name's not *Cho*-lay. It's Chloe. *Klo*-ee."

"Now she is talking!" Dhruv yelled. "How can I draw her if she is always talking?"

Mrs. Singh glanced up from her desk at the other end of

the room. She put one skinny finger to her thin lips. "Shhh!" she hissed.

Why, oh why, did I have to be paired with Dhruv Gupta? Why couldn't I at least be paired with another girl? Anvi Saxena has a long neck and straight black hair that falls like a curtain around her shoulders. I'm really good at drawing long necks and straight hair. I have a special technique.

But Anvi was paired with Prisha Kapoor, of course. They were sitting right behind Dhruv, their heads huddled together. Now they were whispering. They peeked over Dhruv's shoulder. Then they giggled.

Alarm bells went off in my head.

"Hey!" I said to Dhruv. "Hey, let me see!"

I reached for Dhruv's paper, but before I could grab it, he had twisted it out of my reach.

"Hey, what did you do to me?"

I grabbed again. This time I got one end of the paper. Dhruv was still holding tight to the other end. I pulled hard and Dhruv lost his grip. As the paper slipped out of his hands, he fell backward onto the floor.

I looked down at the paper.

I gasped.

Oh my God.

It was me. But I looked like some kind of nutso porcupine with beady eyes, buckteeth, and hair that stuck straight up from my forehead like a row of quills.

It was my hair! Everyone hated my hair!

Before I even knew what I was doing, I had crushed the paper into a ball, pulled the window open, and thrown the ball of paper as far as I could. It hit the roof of the jungle gym in the playground and then bounced down the slide, landing in the bowl of dirt at the bottom. A crow swooped down and pecked at it.

"Mrs. Singh!" Dhruv shrieked from his spot on the floor. "Mrs. Singh!"

Sitting alone at my desk in the middle of the empty classroom, my back to the door, I could hear the shrieks of my classmates as they ran around outside during second break. I wasn't even allowed to read. I was supposed to be thinking about what I had done.

I nibbled at a hangnail on my pinkie. According to the clock on the wall, I had been sitting here for thirteen minutes. It felt like an hour at least. Maybe two.

Whenever I get in trouble, my mom—remember, she's an investigative journalist—tells me to "get to the source." And so I tried to think backward.

I was in trouble because I threw Dhruv Gupta's picture out the art room window.

I threw Dhruv Gupta's picture out the window because he had drawn my head all ugly.

He drew my head all ugly because my mom had cut my hair.

My mom cut my hair because I had colored it black.

I colored it black because I wanted to look like the other girls at Premium Academy.

I wanted to look like the other girls because I live in India and I go to Indian school.

I live in India because my parents moved me here.

So technically, this detention was my parents' fault.

My parents—they were the ones who had brought me to this hot school in this hot country where, even though I wore the same tan uniform and black shoes as everybody else, I stood out like a piece of peppermint in a bowl of licorice. It wasn't fair. If only I had dark hair like Anna's. If only I were neat like her. If only . . .

I put my head down on my desk, resting my cheek on its sticky plastic surface. One tear slipped out of the corner of my eye and sat trapped there for a moment until it spilled over the bridge of my nose and across my cheek. I didn't even bother to wipe it away.

I closed my eyes. It wasn't fair. I am a blond girl. I am an American girl. I shouldn't even be here.

The fan whirled above me, ruffling my porcupine hair. Suddenly, I felt very, very tired.

Before I even opened my eyes, I could already feel another person in the room. I sensed the weight of a gaze on my face.

I opened my eyes.

A girl was standing by the window, watching me.

In my two months at Premium Academy, I had never seen this girl before. Even though she was in uniform like everyone else, I could tell there was something different about her. Maybe it was her hair, which was shiny and hung in thick black braids like ropes down both sides of her face. The braids were tied with big navy-blue bows at the ends, all the way down by her waist. Only the littlest girls at Premium Academy wore their hair like that.

This girl seemed shorter than the other kids in Class Five, and skinnier, too. And there was something funny about her uniform. Her shoes were too big. They stuck out like ducks' feet. Her skirt was too short; two knobby black knees poked out from beneath the hem. And while her shirt was ironed—I could see sharp creases along the sleeves—it had clearly been ripped and then sewn back up at the shoulder. The brown stitches stood out like a scar on the tan fabric.

The girl cocked her head toward the window.

"Dekho," she said.

I shook my head. Ms. Puri had been clear—I wasn't to move from my desk. I was to sit alone for the entire break to reflect upon what I had done.

The thought of Ms. Puri made another tear slip from the corner of my eye. What if Ms. Puri didn't like me anymore? Just last week, when my mom came in for her parent-teacher conference, I overheard Ms. Puri telling her that I was a "real firecracker." She said it in a laughing voice, but now I wasn't so sure. Was that a good thing—like I light up the sky with bright colors? Or maybe a bad thing—like I am noisy and make people jump?

"*Dekho,*" the girl said again. This time she pointed out the window.

I shook my head again. I was staying put.

Then the girl spoke in English: "Come. Look."

Now, you have to understand, I was brought up to be polite. I didn't want to seem rude to this brand-new girl, so I stood up. I would just take a quick glance, then go right back to my desk.

When I got to the window and looked in the direction the girl was pointing, I saw a dog—a mangy, short-haired, gray-and-brown street dog, the kind that lazes around in the road all day, dozing in pockets of sun, and then runs in packs at night, barking and fighting. These kinds of dogs are all over Delhi. This particular one was sleeping, head on its paws, under a tree by the edge of the cricket pitch.

"That's it?" I said. "A plain old dog?"

I was standing right next to the girl. I could smell her. She smelled like Indian cooking—fried onions and spices. Her skin was so dark that the whites of her eyes looked practically blue.

Now she was grinning, and before I could stop her, she put the pointer fingers of both hands in the corners of her mouth and let out a piercing whistle. The dog sprang to its feet but stayed under the tree, wagging its tail furiously. It let out a short bark.

"Are you crazy?" I yelled. I grabbed both the girl's wrists, pulling her fingers from her mouth. "You're not supposed to be here! You'll get me in trouble!"

That's when Ms. Puri walked into the room. I froze, my hands still gripping the strange girl's wrists.

"I—I . . . ," I sputtered.

But then a strange thing happened. Instead of scolding me, Ms. Puri smiled. "So I see you've met Lakshmi," she said. Then she winked. "You are not the new girl anymore, Chloe."

Chapter 4

In America, when a new kid joins the class, everybody makes a big fuss. Maybe the kid's parents come to drop them off. Introductions are made. Everybody goes around the room, saying his or her name. Then the new kid has to stand up and say where they're from and what their favorite movie or flavor of ice cream is, and then the teacher picks a buddy for them so that they feel more comfortable on their first day.

At Premium Academy, there's none of that. On my first day, both my parents walked Anna and me through the school gate where the principal, Mrs. Anand, was standing in a dark green sari, telling students to hurry up. At first, I thought she was there to greet us specially. It was only later that I realized she stands out there every morning before assembly. It's part of her job.

"Today is your first day?" Mrs. Anand said. It seemed like maybe she had forgotten.

"Yes," Mom said. "We are so looking forward to meeting the girls' teachers—"

"I will do the needful," interrupted Mrs. Anand. She held out her hand to me, but I kept firmly gripping Mom's.

"We were hoping—" Dad began.

"We are a big girl, now, aren't we?" Mrs. Anand said, peering down at me.

It really bugs me when grown-ups do that—talk as though they're kids, too, when they are obviously not. There was no "we" in this situation. There was just *me.* I was the only one being sent off to a new school in a new country where I knew exactly nobody. (Well, the only one besides Anna, but she doesn't count because she's older and she's like those chameleons in the rain forest, changing her color to match a new environment.)

Mom squatted down so she was eye level with me. "You can do this, Chloe," she whispered. Her voice was so full of hope that all I could do was nod and let go of her hand.

Lakshmi's parents didn't walk her into class on her first day either. She wasn't introduced. She didn't get assigned a buddy. She simply joined the rest of us as though she'd been there all along. It was like a single minnow joining a school of fish— you start swimming in the same direction and pretty soon, you blend in.

Except that Lakshmi didn't blend in. She stuck out. There was something about her that was different. I could see it in the way the other kids gave her extra space. They didn't cram in close to her, whispering, touching her hair, or tugging on her arm, the way they did with each other. They didn't ask for her mom's mobile number. They didn't steal cookies off her lunch tray, then laugh and put them back.

With me, the girls recognized that I was different—with my blond hair and pink skin, how could they not?—but they still talked to me and gave me toffees and slid their sharpeners over the desk when my pencil tip broke. With Lakshmi, it was like they didn't see her. It was like she wasn't even there.

There was just one other girl—a mousy little girl named Meher whom I honestly hadn't noticed before—and she latched onto Lakshmi like Lakshmi was some kind of life raft. I mentioned that Lakshmi was small and skinny, right? Well, standing next to Meher, even Lakshmi looked normal, that's how scrawny Meher was. She was like this skinny shadow of Lakshmi, sliding around silently beside her.

Later that first day, during dance class, Mr. Bhatnagar gave Lakshmi one long scan, head to toe, frowned, and without saying a word, pointed to the corner. Lakshmi's face didn't change. She just sat down cross-legged on the floor where he had pointed. Every time I glanced over, she was watching the lesson, her big black eyes following every move. I could see her lips counting out the steps. One foot bounced to the rhythm. But she never joined the class. At the end, she stood up from her spot and filed out with everyone else.

In the library afterward, I looked up from my book and

realized Lakshmi wasn't there. Her little shadow, Meher, was missing, too.

"Where's that new girl?" I whispered to Anvi. We were sitting at the same reading table.

"Huh?"

"The new girl—the one with the braids—where is she?"

Anvi rolled her eyes. "You mean Stinky?" she said. "She smells like the kitchen!"

Prisha let out a giggle. "Maybe her mama's a cook."

"Did you see all the oil in her hair?" Anvi said. "It was practically dripping!"

I was starting to wish I hadn't said anything.

"She's been taken for tutoring, you idiots." Drippy-nosed Dhruv was sitting at the table next to ours. He stared at me over the top of his *Young Engineers* book. "They get extra help with English, you know."

"Oh," I said. Who did he mean by "they"?

Anvi and Prisha looked wide-eyed at each other and then burst into giggles. They get that way around boys.

If you are starting to think that Anvi is a little bit mean, you're probably right. Even I had realized that. But I'm telling you, it's like she had cast a spell over all the girls in Class Five. Everybody wanted to be her friend. One day, she came to school wearing this brand-new Kipling backpack. It was a shiny petal pink and it had a pink baby monkey charm hanging from it by a short silver chain. And what do you know? A couple of weeks later, there were petal-pink Kipling backpacks with monkey charms all over Premium Academy. That's when Anvi stopped wearing hers.

Sometimes, lying in bed at night, when I couldn't fall asleep, I would wonder: Was I just another "cool" thing that Anvi had added to her collection? Anvi had asked me for Mom's phone number. She said maybe I could come over to her house one day after school. When she said that, my heart had soared—Anvi Saxena wanted to be friends with *me*!—but then, lying in bed at night, I would stew over it. What if I did go to Anvi's house and then all my newness wore off? What happened when Anvi realized that I was just plain old me?

Back in Boston, I never worried about this kind of stuff. I had my best friend, Katie Standish, and a bunch of other girls I grew up with. We walked our dogs together and baked cookies and played board games. Our moms drank coffee. I never thought about whether we were friends or not. We just were.

Maybe that's why Lakshmi pinged on my radar during her first day at school. Maybe it's because just two months ago, it was me who was the new girl at Premium Academy, standing alone in a corner of the playground, desperate for someone to come up and ask me to play. And then Anvi did come up and it was like a dam broke—all the other girls rushed in.

But no one was doing that for Lakshmi.

During third break, Lakshmi sat alone—I don't know

where mousy Meher was—on a bench under the banyan tree, watching the rest of us with those big black eyes of hers. She swung her skinny legs back and forth, back and forth like metronomes, looking quite content. Her hands lay loose in her lap. When I walked close to her, pretending to look for hopscotch rocks in the roots of the tree, I could have sworn I heard her humming.

So maybe I was wrong? Maybe she didn't want new friends after all?

Maybe she wasn't like me?

Chapter 5

Mom was not at pickup. She sent Vijay instead.

I was so quiet that Anna—who doesn't usually notice me—asked what was wrong.

"Nothing," I said.

But the opposite was true. Everything was wrong. In the morning, I had destroyed my hair and made us late. Then Anvi had laughed at Dhruv's picture of me. And then I got detention—which I had to tell Mom about. And now the weekend stretched before me, a long, hot weekend with this many friends to hang out with: 0.

A long, hot weekend of being cooped up inside, trying to play Monopoly with Dad while Lucy pulled the pieces off the board and stuck them in her diaper.

Back in Boston, I lived for Fridays, when school was over. Here in India, I dreaded them.

"Suit yourself," Anna said.

Even if I tried to explain, Anna wouldn't understand. She *has* friends—friends who call on the weekends and invite her to go to the movies or to the mall. She even got invited to a sleepover once, though Mom wouldn't let her go. Besides, Anna has a thing against Anvi Saxena.

No, Anna would never understand.

As soon as we got home, I went straight to my room to strip off my school uniform and put on my weekend one—a pair of oversized athletic shorts and my favorite faded navy-blue T-shirt with BOSTON RED SOX, WORLD CHAMPIONS in swirly writing across the chest. A surprise was waiting for me. There, lined up in a row on the bedspread, were three stretchy headbands: one gold, one black, one navy blue.

There was also a note scribbled on a yellow Post-it:

For my favorite porcupine. Tomorrow will be a better day. Love, Mommy

I held the Post-it for a minute, then folded it up and put it in the shoe box I keep under my bed. I picked up the blue headband and walked over to the mirror. If I arranged the strip of fabric just right, it covered all the porcupine hairs, flattening them against my hairline. I smiled at my reflection and then ran to Mom's office. But she wasn't there. Anna was there instead. She had already installed herself at Mom's writing desk, her schoolbooks arranged in four neat piles before her. She had laid out her colored pencils in one long row and was getting her sharpener out of her pencil case.

Anna likes all her pencils to be exactly the same length, their points like perfect colored cones. She sharpens obsessively.

"Where's Mom?" I asked.

Anna held up a Post-it note by way of an answer. It read:

A: Had to run to intvu. Don't let C eat whole jar of Nutella! Back by 7. XO M

"Cool!" I said. "Now we get to watch TV!"

Wordlessly, Anna handed me another Post-it:

When C asks, the answer is NO TV.

The *NO TV* part was underlined three times.

"Rats."

I dropped onto the couch and kicked at the leg of the coffee table. "Will you play a game with me?"

Anna didn't look up from her sharpening. "You know I can't. I have to do my homework. And *please* stop kicking the table."

"It's Friday afternoon," I protested. "No one does their homework on Friday afternoon!"

"I do," Anna said. She placed the last pencil back in the row, then smoothed her skirt—she was still in her school uniform—and tucked in her chair. "So if you don't mind . . ."

Anna doesn't like to have any distractions while she works, and I count as a major distraction.

I picked at some crusty stuff on the sleeve of my T-shirt. "But what am I supposed to do?" I whined.

Anna glared at me. "I don't know, Chloe," she snapped. "Just think of something that's not in this room!"

I gave the table one last kick. "I'll go make myself a sandwich."

"Not too much Nutella!" Anna called behind me. "And shut the door!"

I left it wide open.

When I went into the kitchen, Dechen was seated cross-legged on the floor, an enormous bowl of chopped raw meat glistening beside her. Another bowl held a fat lump of dough. Dechen was pulling off nuggets of dough, rolling them out on a wooden board into flat, saucer-sized disks, then stuffing them with the meat and folding them into half-moons. She crimped the edges of the dumplings expertly. When she smiled up at me, her fingers didn't stop moving—roll, stuff, fold, crimp; roll, stuff, fold, crimp. There was a smudge of flour on her cheek.

"Klow-ay!" she greeted me. "You home from school!"

Momos! I replied. Dechen's dumplings are my all-time favorite dinner.

"I make specially for you," she said, and grinned. "How many you eat today?"

"Thirty!"

Dechen gasped in mock horror. "No, no." She shook her head. "Then you too fat, like Dechen." She held her arms over her head and shook them so that the fat wobbled back and forth like a turkey wattle. "Is better I make you five."

"Five?" I protested. "Lucy can eat five!"

Dechen cackled. "I joking you. You no worry. Dechen make you lot of *momos*."

When we first moved to India, Mom realized she would have to hire a cleaning lady, as well as an ayah—a nanny—to help take care of Lucy while she worked, but she was adamant about not having a cook.

Dad tried to reason with her. "This isn't Boston, Helen," he said. "There's no Whole Foods that you can dash over to at six to pick up a roast chicken."

Mom gave him a hard look. "I've always cooked dinner for our family," she said.

Dad could have argued that store-bought ravioli with Prego sauce does not count as cooking, but he didn't.

It took Mom less than a week to capitulate, which means give up. There were too many challenges—the taps ran out of water, the gas canister ran out of gas, the vegetable vendor ran out of vegetables. ("You wait monsoon," he said as Mom paid for one tiny bunch of limp salad greens and one wrinkled cucumber. "We're supposed to wait until it rains to buy our food?" Mom said. He shrugged and turned back to his newspaper.)

Then we all got Delhi belly.

Turned out, Mom hadn't soaked the limp greens and the wrinkled cucumber in chlorine before chopping them up into our dinner salad.

"How was I supposed to know I had to sterilize every

goddamn vegetable?" she groaned from her spot over the toilet bowl. "I mean, who does that?"

Dad was doubled up on the bed. "You . . . are . . . never . . . cooking . . . again," he said.

The very next morning, the doorbell rang. When Mom opened the door, Dechen was standing there, smiling. She had heard from the security guard across the street that we were looking for help.

"I all-rounder," she announced. "I do cooking, I do cleaning, I do baby. I do everything good for you."

"Word sure travels fast around here," Mom muttered.

"You're hired," Dad said.

I pulled the Nutella jar out of the kitchen cabinet and grabbed a spoon from the drawer.

"Tsk-tsk," Dechen clucked. "Your mama tell me no Nutella today."

"Well, I don't see her here right now," I grumbled.

Dechen's hands stopped working for a moment. "Why you so angry, Klow-ay?" she said. "You beautiful girl. You must be beautiful on inside, too."

I should explain: Dechen is Tibetan. Well, she was born and raised in a Tibetan refugee camp in southern India, and while she has spent every one of her twenty-three years in India, not Tibet, she feels completely Tibetan, not Indian. She dresses in T-shirts and jeans—never a sari or a *salwar kameez*—and she wraps Tibetan shawls around her waist.

Her face is round and smooth. She has fat cheeks that flush pink when she stirs things over a hot stove. And she is a Buddhist. So she's always telling me to calm down, which usually has the opposite effect.

"I am *not* beautiful on the inside *or* out," I snapped. I slammed the Nutella jar down on the counter but not before stuffing one glorious, goopy spoonful into my mouth.

"Klow-ay!"

I could hear Dechen calling my name, but I was already out the front door and down the stairs. I pushed open our gate and crossed the street to the park.

In case you've never been to Delhi and you are imagining it as one traffic-jammed parking lot, let me take a moment to explain that—at least where we live, which is a pretty fancy part—it's actually quite green.

Our neighborhood is mainly three-story houses, one apartment per floor. We're the jam in the sandwich—the middle floor, which Indians call the "first floor" instead of the second, just to make things more confusing. Most ground-floor apartments have a little patch of garden out front and a lot of top-floor apartments have roof gardens. In our neighborhood, there's also a community garden about the size of a soccer field every couple of blocks. Some are dry and dusty with plastic bags and *paan* wrappers strewn about, but some are pretty nice. The nicer ones are taken care of by *malis* who spend a lot of time lying on benches and napping, but also squat in the grass, trimming it with scissors. (I kid you not.) They also drag black rubber hoses around to water the grass with something that smells a lot like pee. (Dad says it might actually *be* pee. Yuck.)

In our park, the head *mali* keeps an enormous pair of metal shears tucked into his belt in case he comes across a leaf that's out of place. He's bossed around by two old aunties who live in a concrete bungalow across from the main entrance to the park. The aunties like the bushes neat-neat-neat, so they're out there at six every morning in their saris and sneakers, squawking at the *mali* to trim-trim-trim. This upsets me a bit. I like my trees big and messy—towering elms and broccoli-shaped oaks. The trees in our Delhi park look like kids with fresh haircuts.

At least there are the champa trees. Those are my favorites. They're so big, the *mali* can't reach the upper limbs to cut them. And they have low, knobby branches, so they're easy to climb. If you climb high enough, you reach the canopy, which is so thick with dark green, waxy leaves, you're pretty much hidden. Sometimes, after school, I bring a book and a bag of potato chips and camp out up there for a while.

The champa flowers look like they're carved out of Ivory soap. They're thick and creamy white with bright yellow centers, and they smell so good. Sometimes I close my eyes and put a flower right underneath my nostrils and take a long sniff. In that moment, I'm back at Nana and Grandpa's house on Cape Cod, hiding in the honeysuckle bush by the old toolshed. I can hear the waves crashing. I can hear the seagulls crying as they try to break crabs open by dropping them on the dock. I can almost taste the sea.

Then I open my eyes and see the plain old crows in the dried-up park and I realize: I'm still living in Delhi.

When I got to the park, there were a bunch of boys playing cricket by the broken swings. It was really hot, and sweat was pouring down their faces and making their shirts stick to their backs in dark splotches. They were all staring at the bowler in intense concentration as he started jogging toward the batsman, with the ball in his hand.

I was skirting the cricket area, heading for the champa trees, when Dechen's voice rang out, "Klow-ay! Klow-ay!"

I stopped to turn and look up toward our balcony, where Dechen must have been standing, calling to me, and that was when *CRAAACK!*

I fell to my knees, both hands pressed against my face. Tears filled my eyes as the pain rushed through me. I felt a wetness on my fingers.

Then, out of nowhere, a girl was crouching beside me. She was trying to pry my fingers away. I looked up and I recognized her—those huge dark eyes with the whites so white, they're practically blue. It was the new girl from school. Her lips were moving. She was saying something to me but I couldn't hear her—there was too much ringing in my ears. The ringing was so loud, I couldn't hear anything. I wanted to say something to the girl, to tell her I recognized her from school, but the words wouldn't come out. I couldn't seem to speak. And then, just as I felt a darkness swelling up over me, I saw Dechen's round face, bright pink from running.

"Dechen," I whispered. And the world went black.

When I woke up, I was in bed.

Mom was sitting in a chair beside me. Her laptop was balanced on the foot of my bed and she was leaning forward, typing at an awkward angle. She was concentrating hard, her eyebrows knitted together. She chewed on her bottom lip as the computer keys went clickety-clack.

"Mom?" I whispered. My throat felt dry. I licked my lips.

She looked up. "Hey there, pumpkin." She put her laptop on the floor and scooted her chair up toward the head of the bed, leaning over to place a cool hand on my hot forehead. "How you feeling?"

"Water," I whispered. She nodded and handed me a glass from the night table. When I took a sip, pain shot through the left side of my face.

"What happened?" I asked.

"You got hit with a cricket ball," she said. "Got you on the left cheek. Luckily, Dechen saw it all from the balcony. And there was a girl from your school there. . . ."

"Lakshmi," I said. I glanced around the room, as though expecting to find her there. "Where is she?"

Mom shrugged. "I don't know, sweetie. I wasn't home when it happened, but Dechen said she wouldn't come in."

Mom was silent for a moment; then she took my hand. "I'm so sorry, Chloe. I should have been home. I was at an interview. I . . ."

"It's okay, Mom," I said. "I'm okay."

Mom leaned back in her chair. "Daddy's on his way home from the airport. When he gets here, we'll take you to the hospital. You blacked out and you might have fractured your cheekbone. We'll need some X-rays."

"No," I said. I pulled myself slowly to a seated position. "See? I'm fine."

The door inched open and Dechen's big, round face poked into the room, Lucy's little one glued right next to hers. When Dechen saw me sitting up in bed, she rushed over and hugged me tight to her chest, rocking me back and forth, Lucy squished between us.

"Ouch!" I protested, but I squeezed her back anyway.

"Thanks God!" Dechen said. She pinched my good cheek between her fingers. "Thanks God you alive, or else who eat all the *momos* I cook today?"

"*Momo!*" Lucy echoed in her little baby voice. "*Momo!*"

And then, even though it hurt my face, Mom and Dechen and I all began laughing at the same time.

Chapter 6

That night, Mom broke open a new pack of tea lights, Dad got two bottles of beer and one carton of apple juice from the bottom shelf of the fridge, and we threw ourselves a *momo* party. It hurt a little when I chewed, but I still managed to break my personal record: twenty-three *momos*. When I dribbled soy sauce down my T-shirt, Mom didn't say anything, she just handed me a paper napkin and pointed.

There was vanilla ice cream for dessert. It was the local brand, Mother Dairy. Usually Anna complains—it's too full of artificial flavors and emulsifiers; she likes to keep her body clean and pristine, outside *and* inside—but even she must have been feeling the family glow, because I saw her sneak seconds.

Once we had all finished, a satisfied lull settled over the table. Dad leaned back in his chair and rubbed his hands on his full belly in his relaxed, Friday-night pose.

"So who's this savior of yours, this Lakshmi?" he asked.

I shrugged. "Don't really know. She showed up at school today," I said. "She's new." I scraped the bottom of my ice cream bowl with my spoon. "She's a little strange."

"What do you mean 'strange'?" Mom said.

My mom is always doing that: repeating what I say and then asking me what I meant. I guess it's the journalist in her. I find it pretty annoying. Can't I just say what I want and not have to explain it all the time?

"I just mean strange," I said.

"Elaborate, please," Mom said.

I rolled my eyes. "You wouldn't understand."

"Try me."

"Well, no one really talks to her. No one tries to be friends with her. And she looks kinda different." I hesitated, searching for more specific evidence. "Anvi says she smells."

"She's EWS," Anna said quietly.

I turned to Anna, surprised. "What?"

"She's EWS: economically weaker section." Anna looked at me. "It means she's poor."

"Oh," I said.

Mom and Dad exchanged a glance over the table.

"What do you know about this, Anna?" Dad said.

Anna started folding her napkin, matching the corners up, then running her index finger slowly along the crease.

"You know how I'm a uniform monitor?" We all nodded.

"We had a meeting today. There are some EWS kids who don't . . . um . . . who *can't* comply with all the uniform regulations. So we had a meeting to decide what to do about it. Lakshmi's name came up."

Mom tilted her head to the right—her investigative reporter pose. "These EWS kids, they don't have the money to buy uniforms?"

"Mostly," Anna said. "So we're offering them uniforms from the lost and found. But I guess some parents won't take them. They're too proud or something. Others do, but then the kids end up with uniforms that might be, like, faded or re-hemmed or have missing buttons or whatever." Anna gave a little shudder at the thought. "They don't always look . . . proper."

"Lakshmi's skirt is too short and there's a rip on her sleeve," I volunteered.

"And that's why she's quote-unquote strange? And that's why the other kids are refusing to befriend her?" There was an angry bite to Mom's voice.

Let me take a minute to explain: my mom's parents (my nana and grandpa—the ones on Cape Cod) used to be hippies, which means that they had really long hair and walked around barefoot and believed that everybody is equal and should love everybody else. They taught my Mom to care about Issues of Social Justice, which is, like, how people treat each other. She gets really worked up about stuff like that.

"She does have a friend," I protested. "There's this girl Meher—"

"She's EWS, too," Anna said.

Mom's face was turning red.

"Helen . . . ," Dad said.

"No, David," Mom said. "I will not have such talk at my dinner table—"

"Take it easy. Chloe had an accident today. She doesn't know any better."

"Take it easy? I will *not* take it easy!" Mom banged her fist on the table, making the chopsticks—and all the rest of us—jump. "And she *should* know better. Isn't it bad enough that the girls are surrounded by daily displays of ostentatious wealth? The 'New India,'" Mom said, and snorted. "How much of that money is made off the backs of the poor? I will not have them engaging in discriminatory behavior toward the economically disadvantaged!"

"Lord, please," Anna muttered. "Not the 'I Have a Dream' speech again."

Dad held his hands up in T-formation in front of his chest—his time-out pose when we all start to bicker.

Mom paused and took a deep breath.

"How about we try to explain this to the kids," Dad said.

"I'd like to hear you try," Mom muttered. She took a swig from her beer bottle.

"So, girls," Dad began. He had turned on his lecture voice, the one he uses for colloquiums, which is his fancy word for meetings. (My dad's an economist. His meetings are about money and banks and stuff.)

"A few years ago, the government of India instituted a new law—the Right to Education Act—which said that education is a fundamental right of every child. Every Indian child *must* go to a local school—and it's the government's responsibility to see that they do."

Mom couldn't help herself: "But the government schools are deplorable. It would be a crime to force children—"

Dad held up his time-out signal again and—surprisingly—Mom stopped.

"In Delhi," Dad continued, "the government told private schools, including yours, that they had to start admitting a certain percentage of children who fall under the 'economically weaker section.'"

"Poor kids," I said, trying to be helpful. "They had to take in poor kids."

"Yes, Chloe," Dad said. "Something like twenty-five percent of every incoming class in every private school must be reserved for EWS students."

"Like Lakshmi," I said.

"Like Lakshmi," Dad said.

Mom's eyes were shining. "Can you imagine?" she said. "This could be the beginning of a social revolution in India. New doors of opportunity opening for children whose parents had none!"

"But Lakshmi's not a little kid," I said. "I mean, she's not starting in kindergarten."

"Her dad's the new *mali* at school," Anna chimed in. "They sometimes give places to children of staff."

"That's what I mean!" Mom clapped her hands. "It's simply extraordinary. The daughter of a school gardener sitting next to the daughter of a tycoon!"

"Anvi Saxena's dad is a tycoon," I volunteered. "She brought in a magazine once. It had a picture of him at a party. He was wearing a lavender turban. And it said 'Delhi Tycoon' under the photo." I nodded, pleased with myself.

Dad gave Mom a quizzical look.

"Deepak Saxena," Mom said. "CEO of Saxena Enterprises—the ones building that massive commercial complex out in Noida. You know, with the tallest residential tower in the world . . ."

"Hmm," Dad said, raising his eyebrows. Then he turned to me. "That's a good example, Chloe. Because of this new legislation, you now have a girl worth several billion dollars next to a girl whose dad makes, let's say, a hundred bucks a month."

There was a pause as everyone let this information sink in.

"How much do you guys make?" I asked.

Dad smiled. "That's not something you have to worry about, sweetie," he said. "Let's just say that we're in the middle. We're . . ." He paused, then winked at Mom. "We're comfortably middle class."

"Money . . ." Mom sighed. "What you'll learn, pumpkin, is that money is not so important—"

Dad interrupted her: "Well, as long as you have enough to feed your children and put a roof over their heads and provide them with a decent education . . ."

"What actually matters," Mom continued, "is the way we treat one another." She placed one beer-bottle-chilled hand over mine. "And that's why you need to be nice to Lakshmi."

Huh?

"She's new, right? And it sounds like maybe she's having a little trouble fitting in. Can you do that? Can you help her?"

Suddenly everyone was looking at me: my mom, my dad, my perfect big sister, Anna. And before I knew what I was doing, I was nodding. I was promising to help Lakshmi— the skinny new kid with the little-girl braids and the ripped shirt—to fit in. I knew that was the right thing to do. I mean, I know from recent personal experience how hard it is to be new, and Lakshmi *had* just helped me out in the park. . . . But the truth is, I didn't know *how* to help Lakshmi. I mean, I was still pretty new myself. And I felt like an outsider too. So what was *I* supposed to do?

Even though I'm getting too big for it, Mom and Dad tucked me into bed that night.

"We're so proud of you, sweetie," Mom whispered as she kissed my good cheek.

I knew what she was talking about. She was talking about Lakshmi, about my promise to help her fit in.

Tears welled up in my eyes, but Mom couldn't see them because the light was already out. She moved toward the door.

"Don't be proud!" I wanted to yell after her. "I don't want to help! I can't! I don't know how! All I want is to go back to Boston, where I'm like everyone else and I have real friends and there are no Lakshmis to worry about."

Instead, I turned on my side and pretended to fall asleep.

An hour later, I was still wide awake.

I checked the alarm clock: 10:07. Mom had given me some Tylenol before bed, but my cheek was still throbbing. I touched it and winced. At least she had agreed to hold off on the hospital visit.

I closed my eyes, trying to sleep, but scenes from the day kept whirling through my mind: the scissors slicing my hair off; the little girl in the pink skirt, crossing the road by the slum; Anvi laughing; drippy-nosed Dhruv's balled-up picture soaring through the air; Lakshmi's big black eyes, looming above me as I knelt in the dirt, my hands at my cheek. Then I was back at the dinner table with everyone staring at me and I was nodding my head again, making a promise I had no idea how to keep.

Chapter 7

"Chloe!" Mom was calling me from her office.

"What is it?" I shouted back.

"Don't yell!" she yelled. "Could you come here for a minute?"

I groaned and dropped my book open-faced on the floor. (It was the third Harry Potter—the best one, if you ask me, which you should because I'm kind of an expert; I've read the whole series twice already.) I glanced at my alarm clock: 10:55. I hadn't even brushed my teeth.

When I poked my head through Mom's office door, she was holding her cell phone in both hands, frowning at the screen.

"Any idea what this is about?"

She handed me the phone.

pls send klowe 4 swimmin 2day sax farm chhatarpur

I smiled. "Yeah," I said. "It's for me."

"I gathered that much."

"Oh, right," I said. "You're the investigative journalist."

"Watch the sarcasm, young lady," Mom said.

"Sorry."

Mom sighed. She was wearing her old Barnard T-shirt, which meant she was having trouble writing. It's her lucky shirt. She only wears it when she's stuck on a story.

She reached up and turned my face so that she could inspect my bad cheek. It had gone yellowish purple overnight.

"Ouch," she said. "How's it feel?"

I shrugged. "Not too bad." Then, to change the topic: "I'm kinda hungry."

Mom dropped her hand from my chin. "Pancakes?"

I smiled. "Yeah, that sounds good."

"And while we make them," Mom said, snapping her laptop shut, "maybe you can tell me about this mystery texter who doesn't care to spell or to punctuate."

We headed to the kitchen. I got the eggs and butter from the fridge, while Mom rummaged through the cupboards, looking for the measuring cups.

"So, who's your new friend?"

"It's Anvi," I said. "You know, the girl I mentioned last night? The one with the tycoon dad? She asked me for your number at school. Said maybe her mom would call. They have some big house with, like, horses and a pool." I dumped my ingredients on the counter. "She's really pretty."

"Hence 'sax farm' . . ." Mom was measuring out the flour.

"Is there a problem, Mom?" This was the first invitation I had had from anyone at school—Anna had already gotten five or six—and it had come from Anvi, which made it especially important. It felt like a test.

"Why would there be a problem?" Mom's voice had that sharp edge, like when you tell your parents you were picked for the softball team but they really wanted you to play chess.

I cracked three eggs into the bowl. "One more?"

Mom nodded.

"You know anything about her family?" I could tell Mom was working hard to make her voice sound all casual.

"Not really."

I got a fork from the drawer and started whisking the eggs. There was a pause in the conversation.

"She told me she has cousins in New York City," I said. "She goes there every summer."

"Well, that must be nice," Mom said.

Dad walked into the kitchen.

"Uh-oh," he said, reaching for the coffeepot. "Your mother never thinks anything is 'nice.'" He poured himself a mug, then leaned against the counter. "Need any help?"

Mom was sifting the flour by banging a sieve against her open palm, and banging it a little too hard—flour was snowing all over the counter.

"Maybe I'm missing something"—*bang, bang*—"but I don't quite understand how people expect me to send my eleven-year-old daughter off to their *farmhouse*"—the word came out like a sneer—"when I don't even know them, I've never met them, they've never introduced themselves to me.

I mean, what happened to having coffee first? Or even a plain old phone call, for Christ's sake!"

Dad and I exchanged glances. "You want me to take over for a bit, Helen?" he said.

Mom looked down at her Barnard T-shirt, now covered in flour.

"Yeah, maybe." She sighed.

Dad took the sieve out of Mom's hand and placed his coffee mug into it instead. Then he nudged her toward the kitchen door. "You go write," he said. "We'll get breakfast on the table."

"What's she all worked up about?" Dad turned to me once Mom had left the room. "You have some kind of a playdate?"

I rolled my eyes. "They don't call them playdates when you're eleven."

"Right," Dad said. He started mixing the batter. "Chocolate chips?"

I nodded and reached into the freezer for our stash of Hershey's. (Real chocolate chips are hard to find in Delhi. We got this bag from one of Mom's journalist buddies, who brought it back from Singapore a month ago. We ration the chips, one scoop at a time. If we don't keep them in the freezer, they melt into one big puddle. We learned this the hard way.)

I dropped one precious handful of chocolate chips into the batter. Then I watched as Dad mixed them in, scraping the wooden spoon against the sides of the big glass bowl.

These are the things I miss most about Boston: chocolate

chips, soft toilet paper, sidewalks, artichokes, blueberries, the public library, clean tap water, Ben & Jerry's ice cream, and my best friend, Katie Standish.

Standing there, watching Dad pour the chocolate-flecked batter into the pan, I suddenly really, really missed Katie. It hit me like a wave, that missing. Bang. It knocked me over.

"You okay, honey?"

Dad was looking at me, a metal spatula in his right hand.

"Yeah," I said. I wiped my eyes with my T-shirt.

Dad flipped the first batch. "Saturdays a little tough?"

I nodded.

"Well, it's nice you have a, um . . ." He paused, searching for the right word.

"An invitation," I said. "I have an invitation."

"Yeah," he said. "You wanna go?"

I shrugged. "I dunno."

For weeks, all I had wanted was to get in with Anvi and Prisha. Now here was my big chance and I could already feel it slipping away. I wasn't going to go. I was too chicken.

I picked at some batter that had dripped onto the counter. "I mean, maybe Mom's right and we should get to know the family a little better first?"

Dad lowered the flame. "I'm not sure we're going to, um, be fully compatible with the Saxenas, Chloe," he said. Then he put one hand on my shoulder. "But we can try. We'll do whatever you want, sweetie. And you should do whatever makes you most comfortable today. Do whatever feels right."

I looked down at my bare feet. "I think I might feel more comfortable maybe going a different weekend," I said.

"Okay," Dad said. He took his hand off my shoulder. "That's okay."

And even though nothing had changed—I still had two long, hot weekend days to fill and nothing to fill them with—I felt a little better because I had an invitation. I might not be going, but at least I'd been asked. And that was a start.

Chapter 8

It was Dad's idea to go to Humayun's Tomb that afternoon. Maybe he wanted a little culture, or maybe he thought I needed a change of scenery since I had chickened out on going to Anvi's.

"Let me get this straight—you want us to visit a *tomb*?" I was lying on my bed, reading, when he came into my room. "Like, a place that has dead people?"

Back in the U.S., weekend excursions meant a couple of hours at the Museum of Science or the aquarium. We went hiking. We went for a splash at the pool. Maybe stopped for ice cream. We did not hang out at tombs.

"Not dead *people*. One very important dead person: the emperor Humayun. And it's not just a tomb, it's a mausoleum."

I raised one eyebrow, a trick I'd been practicing in the mirror lately. It was supposed to make me look skeptical, which means grown up. At least, I think that's what it means.

Dad didn't seem to notice the eyebrow thing. "It's one of the greatest historical sites of Delhi, Chloe. It has gardens."

He crossed his arms over his chest and cocked his head at me. "Shreya said you'd like it. She said it's nice."

Shreya is my parents' best friend. She has silver hair that's cut really short, like a man's, and studs that line both her ears all the way to the tippy top; there must be a dozen of them. There's a sparkly one stuck in her right nostril, too. She wears long, colorful scarves and those baggy pants that only circus clowns wear in America but that normal people wear here. She doesn't wear any makeup. And her two front teeth are crooked; they overlap like a door that's slightly off its hinges.

Shreya works for an NGO, which stands for nongovernmental organization, and which she explained to me once: she wants the world to be more fair for more people, but she doesn't trust the government to do it. Plus, she's a big help to Mom with her work. Whenever Mom's confused about something or needs help with Hindi or background for a story, she calls Shreya first.

I like Shreya because she's one of those grown-ups who talks to kids like we're normal people. The first time she came over, I was curled up on the couch in the living room, rereading this Judy Blume book that Mom hates.

"*Please* tell me you're not reading that junk again, Chloe," Mom groaned.

Shreya leaned over to get a look at the cover. "*Blubber's* even better," she said, and winked at me.

You can see why I like her.

Our first week in Delhi, Shreya took Mom and me to buy clothes at Fabindia and books at Bahrisons Booksellers. For lunch, she took us to a hole-in-the-wall, where we gobbled down chicken *kati* rolls, grease dripping from their wax paper sleeves.

Another Saturday afternoon, a couple of weeks later, I was about to drop dead with the sheer boredom of my new, friendless life, when Shreya stopped by. She took one look at my face and said, "You ever try *golgappas,* Chloe?"

Before Mom could protest, Shreya had popped me on the back of her scooter and zipped me around the corner to a grimy little storefront I had never noticed before: Bengali Sweet House. We stood there together, in front of the *golgappa* wallah, while Shreya showed me how to stuff whole puffs straight into my mouth and then crunch down on them, letting the tangy sauce gush over my tongue. I wasn't sure I liked *golgappas,* but I sure liked being there with Shreya.

"Best cure for homesickness there is," Shreya said as we climbed back onto her scooter. I wasn't sure if she meant the *golgappas* or herself, but I had to agree.

Even though Shreya seemed to know everything about Delhi—and seemed to get me, too—I still didn't feel like going to this tomb or mausoleum or whatever it was. I felt like staying home.

"Do we have to?"

Mom and Anna were working in the office. Lucy was napping. The house was blissfully quiet. And I was just getting to the part where Harry meets Sirius Black.

Dad reached down and took the book right out of my hands. "C'mon, kiddo," he said. "Get your shoes."

As soon as Vijay parked the car, we were surrounded.

"Sir-*ji*, you buy postcard! You have most beautiful daughter! You buy postcard!"

Dad grabbed my hand and pulled me through the crowd of vendors pushing postcards and potato chip packets and fans into our faces.

We made it to the ticket counter, only to be accosted again: "You need tour? I give you most excellent tour of this most historical and beauteous of monuments in this most magnificent of countries, this incredible India." The tour guide flashed a tattered ID card at Dad, then leaned close, lowering his voice: "Government-certified. I give you very best price."

"No thanks," Dad said, handing me a ticket and brushing past the tour guide. "C'mon, Chloe."

"This is great, Dad," I muttered, pushing through the turnstile. "Really loving this. Super relaxing so far."

But then we walked through the entry gate, and it was like we had passed into a different world.

Vast lawns spread before us. The sun was already low, casting long shadows across the smooth green grass. It was still hot, but a soft breeze stirred the pom-pom tops of the palm trees that lined the main path. There weren't many people, just a few Muslim families out for early-evening strolls. They nodded at us as they passed.

"It's so . . . so peaceful." When I spoke, it came out as a whisper.

In the distance, a man's voice wailed out over a megaphone. He was singing in a language I didn't recognize.

"The call to prayer," Dad said.

I had no idea the place would be so huge. We couldn't even see the mausoleum because it was hidden by an enormous stone gateway at the far end of the lawns.

There's hardly ever this much open space in Delhi.

Dad took my hand and threaded it through his elbow. We started down the main path, our shoes crunching on the coarse sand.

"So this was, like, the model for the Taj Mahal?"

"Yep." Dad nodded. "Bega Begum had it built for her husband, Humayun, after he died. It was a testament to her love."

"That's kind of creepy. . . ."

"Wait, listen!" Dad was standing stock-still in the middle of the path. Then it came again—a weird meowing sound, kind of like a cat.

I looked at him, confused.

"Peacocks! Here, this way . . ."

Dad pulled me off the path, toward a massive, crumbling archway that led to a separate, enclosed garden.

"Hey, look at this." He was pointing to a set of stairs cut into the archway's inner stone wall.

I peered up the steps. It was pitch black up there and smelled like bats.

"I'm not sure we're supposed . . ."

But Dad had already started climbing. He had to use his hands, the steps were so steep. "Come on, Chloe," he called back to me from the dark. "Where's your sense of adventure?"

When I came out at the top of the stairs, Dad was standing right at the edge of the high stone wall, gazing out over the view. The mausoleum spread before us. Its walls, made of sandstone, glowed pink in the setting sun.

I had to admit, it was seriously beautiful.

Dad pointed. A little farther along the wall, a group of peacocks were strutting around, eyeing us warily. They were so close I could see the tops of their blue crowns bobbing up and down and the iridescent eyes on the ends of their tail feathers glimmering.

We sat there for almost an hour, Dad and me, legs dangling off the side of the stone wall, listening to the prayers and watching the peacocks strut. A group of ladies sat in a loose circle in the garden below, their jewel-colored saris fanned out around them on the grass. When the wind stirred the trees, flowers showered down on them, which made the ladies turn their faces up and laugh.

As the sun dimmed, the reflecting pools in the garden around the mausoleum turned silver. The moon rose in the darkening sky. The peacocks meowed.

I'm not kidding: it was like a real-life fairy tale.

Before we knew it, a guard was walking through the grounds, waving people toward the exit.

Dad held my hand on the way out. We hadn't done that in a while, but it didn't bother me a bit.

The same guide was still there, leaning against the wall by the exit, a clay cup of chai in his hands. He grinned at us amicably.

"I tell you it most beauteous monument. Now you believe me, *na?* Next time you take guide."

In the car, on the way home, Dad put his arm around my shoulder and I leaned into him, my head resting against his chest. We didn't need to talk.

"So, how was it?" Mom asked when we walked in.

"It was great." I smiled. "It was really great."

Chapter 9

That night after dinner, Dad arranged a Skype date for me with Katie. It took a long time to get everything set up, so I was kind of amazed when Katie's face finally floated up on the iPad. She looked different on-screen. Her nose was bigger and her skin seemed really pale; her freckles stood out like polka dots. It was morning there, so she was still in her pj's. I had already finished my whole day.

"Oh my God, how are you?" Katie said. "How's India?"

My mind went blank. *How's India?* How was I supposed to answer that?

I looked out the window at the park across the street, baking in the night heat.

"Um, it's hot," I said. "It's really, really hot."

"Oh." Katie sounded disappointed, sort of like, *Really, is that the best you could come up with?*

"But is it cool?" Katie said. "Not cool like temperature—cool like interesting?"

"Yeah," I said. "It's definitely interesting."

I thought about telling her about Humayun's Tomb—about sitting on the wall with Dad, watching the sun set over the gardens—but the words didn't come.

I searched my brain. What was there to say? I mean, how could I explain India? How could I explain the whole place? Everything in Delhi was the opposite of Boston—the heat and the smells and the noises and the colors and the tastes. Everything was totally different.

"There was a snake charmer in the park the other day," I ventured.

"Really?" Katie said. "Oh my God, that's so cool! Did you touch a snake?"

"Um, no," I said. (I had only seen the guy from the living room window. Dechen had pointed him out. He was napping on a park bench, his basket of snakes beside him.)

"Oh," she said. "Still."

"Yeah," I said.

There was a long pause.

"There are lots of cows on the streets," I said. "And sometimes we see monkeys."

"Wow! Do you feed them peanuts?"

"No," I said. "They sit on the back of this guy's bicycle. He dresses them up in these little outfits—a boy and a girl. He asks for money and then he'll make them dance."

"That's so cute!" Katie said.

I didn't tell her the monkey man was really skinny with dirty hair and hungry eyes and that he had the monkeys attached to the bicycle by chains around their necks. When he biked past our house, I'd hide behind the curtain or else he'd spot me, park his bike in the middle of the street, and rattle the monkeys' chains while he yelled up, asking for money.

"What's going on in Boston?" I said.

That's when Katie launched into a monologue about all the things I was missing out on. Even though I had been in school for two months already, school was just starting up in Boston. And Katie's summer had been a blast. She had been to sailing camp and spent the Fourth of July on Nantucket. She had been strawberry picking twice. And she had learned this new trick—catching crabs by tying raw chicken wings with string, then lowering the chicken into the water and hauling it back up as soon as the crabs clamped down on the bait. Her uncle paid her a quarter per crab. She had already made five dollars and seventy-five cents that way.

"You should try it," she said. "It's super fun—there's this big group of camp kids who do it together on the Cape—"

"There's no ocean here," I said flatly.

"Oh, right."

There was another long pause.

"But I did see an elephant once. . . ."

The conversation went on like that for a while, with Katie telling me about something really fun she did back home without me and then me telling her some exotic-sounding detail about life in India. I told her what I thought she wanted to hear—about the India from storybooks with camels and turbans and ladies in saris.

None of it was lies. I mean, most ladies here *do* wear saris. And we *did* take a road trip through Rajasthan where we saw men in bright turbans hitching camels to carts along the highway. What I didn't mention was that our hotel had satellite TV, so instead of going on the "village heritage walk" with Mom, I watched Cartoon Network under the AC.

"It sounds amazing!" Katie said.

"Yeah," I said. I was trying to sound enthusiastic, but mainly, I felt tired. And fake. I felt really fake.

"I think I better go now," I said. "My dad is calling me." (He wasn't.) "This was *so* fun. Let's do it again soon."

"Promise!" said Katie.

"Promise!" I said. And then I hit the red button to make her go away.

Chapter 10

Sunday morning, Dad was the first one to notice I was still in my room while everyone else was up for breakfast. He tapped gently on my door before opening it.

"Everything okay in here, trouper?"

When I didn't answer and just kept staring out the window, he came in and sat on the side of my bed.

"Chloe?" he said. "You okay, sweetie? It's a beautiful morning. Thermostat hasn't even hit one hundred yet." He was acting jokey.

"I can't get out of bed," I said. "I'm sick."

"Is it your cheek?"

I shook my head.

Dad put his hand on my forehead to see if I was running a fever. "Um, I'll check with Mom, but you don't feel hot to me," he said.

"Not that kind of sick," I said.

"Oh," he said, "I see. I'll be right back."

When he came back, he was holding an enormous mug of coffee in one hand. In his other hand was the pink plastic stethoscope from our toy doctor's kit—a toy that used to be my favorite. I hadn't played with it in years; it was Lucy's now.

"Dr. Dad to the rescue!" he announced, but when he tried to put the stethoscope to my chest, I batted it away.

"I'm too old for that," I said.

A look of pain flashed across Dad's face. I immediately wanted to take back what I had said, but it was too late. He had already slipped the stethoscope from his neck. It flopped limp in his hand.

Dad took a couple of long sips from his coffee mug, the rim hiding his eyes. "I'll go get Mom," he finally said. And before I could call him back, he had walked out of the room.

Another fifteen minutes passed before Mom showed up. When she did, she was wearing her Barnard T-shirt over a pair of Dad's old boxer shorts. She had her glasses on and her hair pulled up in a messy knot on top of her head.

"What is it, Chloe?" she said. She kept one hand on the doorknob.

"I'm sick," I said, but my voice came out small and uncertain.

Mom strode to the side of my bed and placed one hand on my forehead. Her eyes were bloodshot. "You don't feel hot."

"Not that kind of sick." My voice was even smaller.

Mom put both hands on her hips. "Well, what kind of sick exactly?"

I hesitated. "I'm homesick."

"Good grief, Chloe!" Mom snapped. "I'm on deadline. I have to produce twelve hundred words on the rotavirus vaccine in the next sixty minutes, so as long you're not presenting with severe diarrhea, I don't have the luxury to give a damn!"

She spun on her heels and marched out of my room, slamming the door behind her.

There was a time, not too long ago, when I thought my mom would actually fall down dead if she didn't turn a story in on time. Turns out, "deadline" is just a figure of speech.

I still had on my Boston Red Sox T-shirt, Friday-night soy sauce dribble and all. I slipped my shorts on. Rather than brush my hair, I pulled a baseball cap over the tangles. Anna was in the kitchen, cutting a mango into neat slices. She glared at me when I opened the fridge and gulped some OJ straight from the carton. I didn't say anything, only grabbed a granola bar from the cupboard.

I could hear Mom pounding on the keys behind the door to her office. Dad was too busy cooing over Lucy in the living room to notice when I opened the front door and slipped out.

I'm not supposed to leave the house without telling anybody, but I really couldn't be bothered. Besides, nobody seemed to care.

Outside, the air was still, hot, and very humid. The sky was gray and swollen with water that refused to fall.

It was only ten o'clock. By noon, it would be one hundred and ten degrees. Sweat beaded on my forehead.

"Stupid monsoon," I muttered as I slipped through the gate to the park. I had never wanted it to rain so badly.

I kicked at a rock in the walking path. It came loose, so I picked it up and threw it. It landed farther down the pavement, skittered a few feet, then slammed into one of the champa trees in a cluster at the center of the park. It felt good. I kicked another rock loose and then threw it at the tree. Then another.

"*Bas!*" a voice said.

I froze, a rock ready to launch in my pulled-back arm.

"*Bas!* Stop!" the voice said. It was a girl's voice. It was coming from the champa trees.

I walked over to the base of the trees and looked up. Way up high—higher than I'd ever dared to climb, up in the uppermost canopy—I could see a pair of feet dangling down. They were bare feet, black on top, brown with mud on the soles.

"Lakshmi?" I said.

A face appeared between the knees that were attached to the feet by a pair of stick-thin shins.

Lakshmi's face grinned down at me.

"Oh," I said. "Hi."

"You come." It wasn't a question, more like a command.

Lakshmi beckoned to me with one hand and as she did, the top of the tree swayed. She grabbed at a branch for balance. "You come!" she repeated.

"I dunno," I said. I'm no chicken, but watching her up there made my stomach go queasy.

"You scared," Lakshmi said. Again, it was a statement, not a question.

I was really not in the mood to be picked on, so I kicked off my flip-flops and hauled myself up onto the lowest branch of the tree next to hers. Mine was a bigger, older tree, so I could climb up to about Lakshmi's height and still be among thicker, sturdier branches. I sat in the V created by a branch, my back against the trunk, my bare feet dangling. I was breathing hard. I didn't dare look down.

Once I caught my breath, I leaned forward and peered through the leaves, trying to get a better look at Lakshmi in the neighboring tree. The foliage was so dense I could only see her feet and shins poking out.

"Lakshmi?"

And then I saw one small brown hand slowly reaching across to my tree. The fingers grabbed hold of the end of my branch, which sagged in response. Before I could yell, "Stop! No!" Lakshmi had swung across to my tree. She was hanging on to the end of my branch, her bare feet curled around it, grasping it from beneath like the three-toed sloth I'd seen on TV once. The branch dipped and right when I was sure that it was going to snap in half—and that she was a goner—Lakshmi started to shimmy herself toward the trunk. Before I knew it, she had flipped herself over the branch and was sitting beside me, grinning like crazy.

"B-b-but . . . ," I stammered. I was gripping the branch so tightly that my knuckles had gone white.

"Hello!" Lakshmi said, and then let out an earsplitting cackle, like she had just told the funniest joke in the world.

"Hello?" I echoed. "Hello? You could have killed both of us! We could have died!"

Lakshmi stopped laughing as quickly as she had started. She pointed at my cheek, which was now eggplant-colored—blackish purple. "You face feeling okay?"

I touched my cheek gingerly, wincing at the tenderness. "Yeah," I said. "I'm okay. . . . And thanks," I added. "Thanks for helping me out the other day."

Lakshmi shrugged. "No issue," she said.

"Hey . . ." I was about to ask her why she hung out in the park so much—if maybe she lived nearby—but she was already scrambling down the trunk. She didn't climb like an American kid—moving methodically from branch to branch—but instead shimmied right down the trunk, Spider-Man-style. In a blink, she was on the ground.

"*Chalo!*" she commanded, beckoning to me from below. "*Chalo,* Chhole!" She cackled again.

Before I could protest—I really did *not* want that chickpea nickname to stick—she was already skipping halfway across the park, her long black braids bouncing off her back.

It took me a while to extricate myself from the tree, and I let out a sigh of relief when my bare feet hit the grass. I slipped on my flip-flops, wiped my sweaty hands on my T-shirt, and then looked around for Lakshmi. I finally spotted her in the far corner of the park, over by the playground. She was squatting, her attention focused on the ground.

Now what?

As I got closer, I could see what Lakshmi was doing. She was petting a dog. It seemed to be the same dog that she had pointed out to me at school, though up close it looked in even worse shape than it had through the classroom window. It was a splotchy mix of gray and brown—like someone hadn't mixed the colors well enough before painting—and it had tufts of fur missing. A pink scar ran along its snout from its left inner eye all the way to its black nose. A chunk the size of a rupee was missing from one ear. It must have been in some vicious fights. It was so skinny, its ribs poked up like speed bumps, but it was strong-looking, too, with a broad, muscular chest. It was lying on its side, groaning with pleasure as Lakshmi scratched it hard behind one ear.

When I came up behind Lakshmi, the dog stiffened and whipped its head up to glare at me. It let out a low, warning *grrrr,* but then Lakshmi whispered, "Shhh," and it lowered its head back down to the dirt and closed its eyes.

"This dog, Kali," Lakshmi said without looking up at me. She was scratching the dog's back with both hands now.

"Is it yours?" I squatted down next to Lakshmi, but kept my hands on my knees. I'm nuts about dogs, but I had promised my parents never to go near street ones. One of the first articles Mom wrote when we moved here was about rabies in Delhi.

Lakshmi shook her head. "My dad say no dog in house. Kali street dog." She looked at me. "You touch?"

I shook my head. "Maybe another time."

But Lakshmi reached over and took one of my hands off my knee and placed it onto Kali's side and held it there. I could feel the dog's heart beating through its ribs: *da-dum, da-dum, da-dum.* Its fur was surprisingly soft—not coarse like I had imagined—particularly compared to Lakshmi's palm, which felt dry and rough against the back of my hand.

"Kali not my dog," Lakshmi said. "Kali my friend."

We spent the rest of the morning playing in the park with Kali, whom Lakshmi had trained to do all kinds of neat tricks: fetch sticks, bark on cue, chase her own tail, roll on the ground. It was only when Kali paused to sniff at the *mali's* dried-up hose that I realized how thirsty I was.

"You thirsty?" I asked Lakshmi.

She gave me a perplexed look.

"Nimbu pani?" I asked, wanting some lemonade myself.

It was boiling hot. Lakshmi's lips were dry. Sweat glistened on her face. She *had* to be thirsty. But she shook her head and then glanced up at the windows to our apartment across the street.

"C'mon," I said, pulling on her elbow. "Let's go get something to drink."

But Lakshmi dug her heels in. She reminded me of Kali now—stick-thin but stubborn and strong.

"Well, I'm going," I announced, and started walking toward the house.

When I glanced behind me, Lakshmi was standing by the gate to the park, watching me. I crossed the street, and when I looked back again, she was following me, on the opposite side of the street. I opened the gate to my house, but Lakshmi stayed on the other side. She was frowning. With one hand, she wrapped and unwrapped the end of one braid around her other hand. Kali had followed her and now lay down, placing her muzzle on Lakshmi's foot.

"C'mon, Lakshmi," I said. I was getting exasperated. "I'm really thirsty. Do you want a drink or not?"

Lakshmi didn't move.

"Can't we at least get some water for the dog?" I said. "Kali's got to be thirsty, right?"

When Lakshmi's eyes lit up I knew I was on to something.

"Help me get water for Kali," I urged.

Lakshmi crossed the street slowly, placing one foot in front of the other like a gymnast walking on a balance beam, but when I held the gate open for her, she froze on the threshold. Her hands clenched and unclenched the hem of her kurta. It was a maroon kurta with gold paisley patterns printed all over it, and it was only then that I noticed that most of the sequins had fallen off and that the olive-green pajama pants Lakshmi wore didn't match.

"You look fine," I said. I was trying to sound reassuring, but Lakshmi scowled.

"No fancy kurta," she said. "No *dupatta*." She shook her head and pointed up toward the apartment. "I can no go your house."

"Are you kidding?" I said. "Look at me!" I pointed at the soy sauce stain on my Red Sox T-shirt. "Seriously," I said. "My parents do *not* care. Like, *not at all*. Actually, I know for a fact that they'd love to meet you. You have nothing to worry about. American parents are . . ." I paused for a moment, searching for the right word. "They're different. They're, um, cool."

Lakshmi looked unconvinced, but before she could protest further, I grabbed hold of her hand and started pulling her up the stairs.

Dad dashed over the moment we walked through the door. He must have been watching us through the living room window.

"You must be Lakshmi!" Dad stuck out his right hand to shake, but Lakshmi just stared at it, confused, till he dropped it back by his side. "I'm David," he said. "And this little rascal is Lucy."

One look at my pesky baby sister and Lakshmi dissolved into mush.

"*Chota* baby!" she exclaimed.

Before we knew it, Lakshmi had taken Lucy right out of Dad's arms and was holding her on her hip. She pinched Lucy's fat baby cheek, which is what Indians tend to do when they meet a cute little kid.

I could see Dad staring at Lakshmi's dirt-encrusted fingernails, now clamped on to Lucy's peachy cheek. He jammed his hands in his pockets, resisting the urge to grab the baby back from her.

Meanwhile, Lucy had curled her fingers around one of Lakshmi's long black braids. She yanked.

"Yeow!" Lakshmi yelped, and we all laughed.

"Okay, enough baby time," I announced. "Let's get some *nimbu pani* and go to my room."

Lakshmi unhooked Lucy's fingers from her braid and handed her back to Dad. She followed me into the kitchen. Anna was standing at the sink, scrubbing her hands with antibacterial soap.

Lakshmi stared at her, awestruck. "You have two sister?" she said.

"Yeah," I said. "Lucky me!"

She didn't pick up on the sarcasm in my voice.

"Three girl?" Lakshmi said.

"Yep. What's the big deal?"

"No one has three girls in India," Anna interjected. "Didn't you know that?"

I shook my head.

"Well, do any of the kids in your class have two sisters?"

I thought for a second and then shook my head again. "I don't think anyone has two anything," I admitted. I had never thought about it before.

"Overpopulation," Anna said matter-of-factly. "In China, most families are allowed only one child. In India, people are *allowed* to have as many kids as they want, but most stop at two. It's a cultural thing. And hardly anyone has two girls because of prenatal sex selection and infanticide—long-standing cultural prejudices against females."

Lakshmi stood there with her mouth open, staring at Anna throughout this speech.

"See ya," Anna said, and walked out.

"In case you were wondering, yes, she is always like that," I said. "She's a lecturer. Gets it from our dad." I had taken two glasses from the cupboard and was squeezing fresh limes into them with my bare hands.

Lakshmi watched me. "I have no sister, no brother," she finally said.

"You're *sooo* lucky." I dumped some sugar, then water, into each glass and gave them a stir. "My sisters are such a pain. I wish I was you."

Lakshmi looked down at the floor.

I bit my lip. What did I know about Lakshmi? What did I know about her family? Her life?

"You want some ice?" I asked, trying to change the subject.

Lakshmi looked puzzled, so I walked over to the freezer and pulled out the ice tray. As I struggled to loosen some cubes from the tray, Lakshmi leaned over and poked one with her finger. Her face spread into a wide grin. *"Thanda,"* she said.

"Cold?" I asked.

She nodded.

"Yeah, they're cold. You want some?"

She nodded again, so I dumped some ice into the glasses and handed her one. She tapped at the ice cubes for a second, trying to sink them, but they just bobbed back up to the surface.

"C'mon," I said. "I'll show you my room."

And that's how it all began.

Part Two

FINDING LAKSHMI

Chapter 11

For whatever reason, Lakshmi and I didn't hang out in
school. There wasn't much free time, but when there was,
I stuck with Anvi and Prisha, while Lakshmi pretty much
did her own thing, unless you count skinny little Meher,
who would slink around behind her. She reminded me of a
kicked puppy, that Meher.

After school was another story. Lakshmi and I met up in
the park almost every day. Even in mid-September, it was
still really hot. There was the occasional rain shower, but no
real monsoon—at least, not the earth-pounding rain I had
heard about—so we baked away under the afternoon sun.
Sometimes we'd sit high in the branches of the champa tree,
where the thick, waxy leaves shielded us a bit. Kali would
put her paws on the trunk and bark at us, annoyed at being
left out.

The aunties had put a new sign up in the park. The top

was in Hindi, but the bottom was in English, and this is what it said:

YOU MAY RELAX HERE
LEAVE YOUR BODY
LOOSE AND BREATH
BE IN A EASY CONDITION
AND TUNE WITH NATURE

I guess that's what Lakshmi and I were doing: tuning with nature. Sometimes when the aunties were sitting on their metal benches, sweating and chanting mantras while their maids fanned them with newspapers, we'd toss champa flowers down at them—not a lot, just enough to make them look around, confused.

When we got too hot, we'd go inside and sneak Cokes to my room. It was Lakshmi who got the ice cubes out of the freezer now.

There's something I'm really good at that I haven't mentioned yet but I'm actually pretty proud of: origami.

It all started back in Boston last spring. It was toward the end of the school year, right after Mom and Dad told Anna and me about moving to India and I was pretty upset. Then the school librarian, Mrs. Rodriguez, gave me a copy of this book *Sadako and the Thousand Paper Cranes,* which is about a twelve-year-old girl in Japan. At first, Sadako is fine and healthy and winning relay races at her school, but then she gets really sick from the atomic bomb. They put her in the hospital and she's dying and then she starts making origami cranes to pass the time. She wants to make a thousand cranes—because that's what Japanese people do when they have a really important wish—but she only gets to 644.

I guess this book got under my skin because right then and there, I decided that I was going to make Sadako's 356 remaining paper cranes (1,000 minus 644 is 356; if you don't believe me, you can do the math). The problem was that I didn't want to start making the cranes and then have to move them all to India—they'd get smashed in the suitcase—so I found the instructions online and just practiced at first. I didn't tell anybody about it, not even Katie.

By the time we were ready to leave Boston, I could make a crane in eight minutes flat. I didn't rush. I wanted them to look really nice.

The day after we moved to Delhi, I started making my 356 cranes. Every day, I would sneak a couple of pieces of paper from Mom's printer—just a couple of pieces a day so that she wouldn't notice them missing—measure them, and cut them into perfect squares. Then I'd make the cranes.

The hardest part was figuring out where to put them. I wanted this to be my secret until I completed all 356. So at first I filled up a couple of shoe boxes, which I hid under my bed. Then I started putting the cranes in a big heap, way up on the top shelf of my closet, behind my winter clothes. But one day I came home from school and Dechen was standing in front of my closet, twirling a crane between her fingers.

"What this?" she said, looking at me. There was a small pile of white printer-paper cranes on my bed.

For some reason, I started to cry. I guess I didn't want to have to stop making my cranes.

The next day, when I got home from school, there was a neat stack of brand-new colored paper on my bed. Not rough construction paper, but glossy paper in jewel colors: ruby and turquoise and emerald green. I didn't even have to cut the paper—it was already in squares.

Dechen never said another word about my cranes, but sometimes—I guess when she had to get something from the top of my closet—I noticed that she had moved the piles around a bit.

One day, during recess, Anvi and Prisha were working on one of their dance routines. I was sitting on the bench, taking notes for them. (I had become the official choreography note taker. Yep, it's about as fun as it sounds.) They sat down for a water break.

"Hey," I said. "Have you guys ever done origami?"

Anvi crinkled her nose. "You mean that stuff that Japanese people do?"

Prisha pushed her eyes up at the corners. "I am Japanese!" she singsonged. Then she grabbed my notepaper and crumpled it into a ball. "Look, an origami rock!" She tossed the balled-up paper to Anvi.

"Hey!" I said. "Those were my notes!"

But Anvi was laughing really hard at Prisha's joke, so I tried to brush it off. I even made myself laugh a little too, though it came out like "huh, huh," not like a real-sounding laugh.

Later that day, right at the end of science class, I heard Prisha telling Anvi the same joke all over again—balling up a worksheet and making her stupid Japanese eyes. This time I didn't try to laugh. I closed my notebook quickly and took a different stairwell to PE.

That afternoon, it was quiet in the house. Lucy was napping. Dechen was in the kitchen, cooking dinner. Mom was out reporting. Dad was at work. Anna had stayed late for some after-school committee or something. Lakshmi and I had met up in the park, but it was too hot, so we had retreated to my bedroom. Now we were lying on our backs on my bed, watching a lizard on the ceiling. He had skittered into one corner and was frozen there, waiting to catch a fly.

Prisha had made her origami rock joke one more time, right at the end of school, which is I guess what made me do it.

"Hey," I said. "You wanna see something?"

"Mmm-hmm," Lakshmi said.

I reached under my bed, pulled out one of the shoe boxes, and removed the top.

Lakshmi's eyes widened. She didn't say anything at first, just reached into the box and picked up one white printer-paper crane. She held it in her palm, just inches away from her big black eyes, and inspected it carefully for a few minutes, turning it every which way. Then she placed it carefully on top of my night table. She picked up another crane and inspected it just as carefully before placing it next to the first one. She went on like this for a while: picking up each paper crane, inspecting it, then putting it down in a neat row on top of the night table.

When she finally spoke, her voice was full of wonder. "You make this, Chloe?"

I nodded.

"You teach me?"

I smiled. "Sure," I said. And then I told her the secret of the cranes, that if you made one thousand of them, you would get your wish.

Lakshmi listened quietly throughout the story. She never laughed at me, not once.

"And you have one wish?" she asked when I got to the end.

I nodded. She didn't ask me what it was. Instead, she rubbed her hands together. "So what we waiting for, *na?*"

Dechen got quiet when Lakshmi was around. Sometimes she'd poke her head into my room unannounced, a scowl on her round face. She checked up on us a lot. Too much.

That afternoon, when she opened the door and saw the paper cranes lined up on my night table, and Lakshmi and me sitting on the floor, folding the jewel-colored paper, Dechen frowned and closed the door without saying a word. I could tell she was upset.

"What's wrong?" I said after Lakshmi went home. "Why don't you like Lakshmi?"

Dechen didn't look up from the ironing.

"Why won't you let her hold Lucy?"

"She Indian girl," Dechen said quietly.

"So?" I said. "In case you hadn't noticed, so is everybody else around here. So are *you*."

Dechen glared at me for a moment. She hates being called Indian.

"Her hair dirty," Dechen said. Her voice was low. "She having the lice?"

I shook my head. I couldn't believe this.

Dechen went back to ironing. "Now I wash pillowcase every day," she grumbled.

The next day, when Lakshmi and I were sitting cross-legged on my bedroom floor, making origami cranes, I snuck a peek at her hair, but I didn't see any specks.

"Um, Lakshmi?"

She looked up.

"Maybe, um . . . maybe we could go to your house one day instead?"

Lakshmi's face twisted into a frown.

"You no like my house," she said. "It small. No TV."

"We don't watch TV here," I said. This was true. When Lakshmi came over, we mainly played in the park. When we came indoors, it was just to take a break from the heat. Neither of us were really indoor people.

"What you want to see?" Lakshmi said. Her voice was tight and angry.

She jumped up. Her hand clenched around her half-finished paper crane, crushing it. "You want to see my house small, your house big? You want to see my house dirty, your house clean? You want to see my house sad, your house happy? You have sister, I don't have? You have baby? That what you want to see?"

"I—I . . . ," I stammered. But it was too late. Lakshmi had already run out of my room.

I heard the front door slam. I rushed to the window. A couple of seconds later, Lakshmi came flying down the stairs and out the front gate. Her stick figure ran down the street.

"Klow-ay? You okay, Klow-ay?" Dechen was standing in the doorway to my room, her face creased with worry. She held Lakshmi's crushed paper crane.

"Now look what you've done!" I yelled.

I knew this wasn't Dechen's fault. I knew it. Still, I couldn't stop myself.

This was my first fight with Lakshmi. I needed someone else to blame. Besides, it was Dechen who had planted a seed of doubt in my brain. She was the one who had mentioned the lice.

"She was my friend, Dechen!" I yelled. "My only *real* friend!"

Chapter 12

The next couple of days, Lakshmi didn't come to the park after school. She kept her distance from me at school, too, but like I said before, things had always been different for us there. It was like some unspoken rule—we never hung out together. I stuck with Anvi and Prisha. Lakshmi stuck with Meher, who was the only other EWS girl in Class Five. Turns out, Meher's mom also worked at the school, and Meher had been at Premium Academy since she was little, which surprised me because her English was pretty bad. Or at least, I assumed it was. I didn't really know, because she hardly ever said a word.

Lakshmi finally showed up at the park about a week after our fight. It was a Tuesday afternoon and it was really hot. I was sitting under the champa tree with a book, trying to read, but it was hard because I kept glancing up every couple of minutes, hoping Lakshmi would appear.

And then there she was.

She had Kali with her and she held something in her hand. When Lakshmi sat down next to me, she placed it in the grass. It was a piece of origami in a shape I had never seen before. It looked like a fortune cookie.

Lakshmi didn't say anything at first. She just picked up a champa flower and started fiddling with it, folding its petals all the way back till she could spear them with their own stems. The flower came out like a little ivory box with a golden center.

"Hey, it's flower origami," I said, and Lakshmi smiled a little.

So we sat there, under the shade of the champa tree, both of us not talking and doing champa origami, when, out of the blue, Lakshmi said, "My mother, she also teach me folding technique." She pointed her chin toward the strange piece of origami sitting on the grass between us. "She work in hospital. She teach me to make sister's hat."

So that's what it was: a nurse's cap.

Lakshmi's fingers kept working, folding the champas' ivory petals back, piercing them with their stems. "She teach me corners on bedsheets."

Lakshmi held one flower in front of her face and twirled it in her fingers. "Her uniform, it all white," she said. "White like champa." Then she picked up the little origami nurse's cap. She put it on top of her head and let go, balancing it. The cap stood out against her black hair like a bright star in a moonless sky. Lakshmi grinned.

"She wear hat like this!"

The origami cap tumbled from her hair onto the grass.

I didn't say anything, just kept doing my flower origami, not looking at Lakshmi, hoping she might say more. I was curious. In the few weeks that I had known her, she had never talked about her family before. Not once.

Lakshmi leaned over and put one hand on Kali, who was splayed out on her side in the shade, sleeping. Lakshmi's hand went up and down with Kali's breathing.

"Outside the hospital, one *didi* sits there. She is—what you say?—*phool* wallah?"

"She's a fool?"

"No, no." Lakshmi let out a laugh. "She not fool. She *phool* wallah. She sell flower, jasmine flower."

"Oh, right," I said. *Duh.*

Lakshmi continued: "She have no teeth. Her mouth dark like cave. Every day, she take one basket full of jasmine flower. She massage my head and then she put jasmine inside my hair." Lakshmi leaned back, resting her head against the trunk of the champa tree, her chin tilted up. She closed her eyes. "It smell so nice. Sweeter than champa."

I cleared my throat. I wanted to get back to Lakshmi's family. I wanted to know more about them.

"So . . . your mom was a doctor?"

I don't know what made me use the past tense. *Was.* I could just tell. Something bad had happened to Lakshmi's mom.

Lakshmi's eyes flew open. She frowned at me. "No, I

already tell you, she sister. Christian Medical College. She do injections. She do bandages. She do blood pressure test. It very good hospital. It even have school for girls. That why my English so good. My mother send me every day to Christian Medical College school for girls. The sisters teach proper British English."

"Oh," I said. I couldn't believe how much Lakshmi was telling me. "Um, so your mom is Christian?" This time I used the present tense. *Is.* I was confused.

Lakshmi nodded. "She Christian with fair skin. Her skin like chai with too much of milk. Every night, she use Fair and Lovely. She put cream all over her face. My father laugh. He say, 'You cannot change crow into egret.' Sometime my mama laugh, too, but if she tired from long day at hospital, she hit him. But he just laugh more."

Lakshmi reached down and pinched a piece of grass between her thumb and index finger, then pulled at it, snapping off its top. Her fingers moved to another blade and snapped its top off, too. Then another and another. *Snap, snap, snap.*

"What else was she like?" I said. I was too scared to ask what I really wanted to know. *What happened to her? Did she leave? Did she die? Was she was? Or was she still is?*

Lakshmi kept clipping the grass. "She have small teeth, like rice. She make *idli* with *sambar.* And every night, she sing 'Amazing Grace' to me when I sleep."

And then Laskhmi closed her eyes again and began to sing, "Amazing grace, how sweet the sound that saved a wretch like me. . . ." Her voice was high and thin. It was strange to hear the hymn in the hot, heavy air of the empty park. The sound seemed out of place, like a white girl in an Indian school.

Lakshmi stopped as abruptly as she had started. "It was big problem, she marry my father. She Christian from Kerala, he black Tamil man."

"So why did she?"

Laskhmi shrugged. "It love match," she said. "My father, he black skin but he handsome one time. And he sing. So much of singing. He sing Bollywood song and my mama laugh or he sing love song and she put her head here." Lakshmi patted her lap. She was quiet for a moment. "He stop singing when she . . ." She paused. "When she die."

I held my breath.

The only sound was the *snap snap* of the grass as she clipped it with her fingers.

"What happened?" I finally whispered.

"Fever," said Lakshmi. "She get high, high fever. Hospital try to help, but fever too high. And then she gone."

I learned the rest of Lakshmi's story over the course of the next few weeks. It came out in dribs and drabs—how her father had stopped singing and stopped eating, how he had gotten the fever, too. All their money went to buy blood and medicine to save him. How he had sold their few belongings in Madurai and bought two sleeper tickets to Delhi, where he had an uncle who he thought might help him find work. How Lakshmi had watched India roll by as the train traveled from south to north—the beaches and palm trees of Tamil Nadu giving way to the flat plains of central India, then the clogged streets of New Delhi. The train journey took forty-two hours. Lakshmi barely slept, she was so excited. And then the hard truth, that the uncle had no job for her father and no place for them to sleep. That Delhi was loud and dirty. On their first night, they slept on the platform at Nizamuddin station. When Lakshmi woke it was because she felt little fingers rifling through her bag, which she had placed under her head as a pillow. She screamed, but it was too late, the street boys were already running away, laughing. They had stolen the last thing of value Lakshmi and her father owned: her mother's wedding ornaments. And the worst part: Her father didn't yell or even cry. He just looked at her with tired, empty eyes. Another thing gone.

Chapter 13

By October, things were going a bit better for me at school. We had been in India for almost four months and I had been at Premium Academy for over three. I still stank at Hindi—that was hopeless—so I dreaded the Hindi and Sanskrit classes. (I'd just sit there, feeling stupid, while everybody else worked.) Science and math were okay, since they were both taught in English. Social studies—where we had just finished the Regional Handicrafts of Andhra Pradesh unit and were starting Flora and Fauna of Temperate Grasslands—was boring, but at least it was taught in English, so I could get what was going on. Oh, and I liked English class. Ms. Puri taught that one and she'd call on me specially. Sometimes, when I spoke up in class, I could even hear my accent changing a little, going all singsong like my classmates'. But then I'd catch myself and switch back to my American accent.

As for Lakshmi, I think school would have been really

tough if she wasn't so clever. I don't mean book smart—she didn't get great grades on science and math quizzes—I mean *clever*. Like, this one day—it must have been about a week or two after she had joined school—we came into the classroom and Ms. Puri had written *WRITING WORKSHOP* in large cursive letters on the blackboard.

"Today, children, we will be trying a new experiment, which is"—Ms. Puri tapped her chalk on the blackboard—"writing workshop. You will be given a half hour to complete an expository piece on the topic 'summer holidays.' You will then break into smaller groups, read your essays out loud to one another, and receive valuable feedback from your classmates."

There were a few titters in the room. Indian kids aren't used to working in teams.

Anvi's hand shot up.

"Yes, Anvi?"

"Ma'am, can we pick our own groups, ma'am?"

"No," said Ms. Puri. "I will be dividing the class into sections."

Anvi scowled. "As long as I'm not with one of *them*," she muttered, loud enough that all the kids around her could hear.

Of course, Anvi was put with Prisha. I was in their group too. As were drippy-nosed Dhruv Gupta and Soumya Singh, who's actually pretty nice. That is, when she doesn't have her nose in a book. Lakshmi was added last. As soon as her name was called, I just knew there was going to be trouble.

Ms. Puri told each group to shove their desks together in order to facilitate collaboration (her words, not mine). That's when Anvi pulled a bottle of antibacterial spray out of her backpack.

"*What* are you doing?" Dhruv said.

Anvi started spraying Dettol all over our desks.

"My mother says that we all need protection *now*." Anvi rolled her eyes in Lakshmi's direction.

Lakshmi crossed her eyes at Anvi.

Ten minutes had passed, but when I looked over at Lakshmi's paper, it was still blank. Lakshmi was staring out the window and chewing on the end of her pencil.

I cleared my throat loudly. When she looked over, I pointed at her blank paper.

"Why aren't you writing anything?" I whispered. "We only have twenty minutes till we have to share."

Lakshmi shrugged. "I can't think what I write," she said. She lowered her voice even further. "I don't know 'summer holiday.'"

Dhruv glanced up from his page. He must have overheard us. "Just start from the beginning," he said to Lakshmi. I guess he was trying to be helpful, but he didn't know anything about Lakshmi's circumstances. I did.

"Like, what did you do in May?" Dhruv prompted. "Or where did your parents take you in June? Where did you go?"

Anvi snorted. "They don't *go* anywhere, Dhruv," she said.

Lakshmi glared at Anvi. Then she bent her head over her paper and started writing furiously.

When it came time to share our work, we took turns reading out loud. Anvi went first.

"This summer we stopped in Europe on the way to New York. First we went to Rome and then to Paris, where I climbed the Eiffel Tower and stayed at the Ritz." She looked up briefly. "It's *so* sad; that's where Princess Di stayed right before she was killed." Her head went back down. "Then we flew to Manhattan. We stayed with my American cousins and did *lots* of shopping. After two weeks, Papa took us all to Universal Studios and it was *so* much of fun! Last year we went to Universal Studios in California, but this one was *so* much better because it was in Florida and . . ."

I looked down at my paper. Compared to Anvi's glamorous summer, mine was starting to seem pretty lame. To be honest, it *had* been pretty lame. We moved to India before school in Boston was even over. I missed the last week, which is the most fun part of the whole entire year. And then I had to start Indian school just a few weeks later. Some summer vacation, right?

Nana and Grandpa were the only good part, really. In May, when Mom and Dad were busy packing, Anna and I got to have weekend sleepovers at their house on Cape Cod. They took us to the ice cream parlor for chocolate fudge sundaes and to the public library for arts and crafts. One night we built a bonfire on the beach. It was chilly and the sand was damp, but we lay on our backs, close to the fire, and made up constellations like the Xbox 360 (mine), the violoncello (Anna's), and the one-tusked walrus (Grandpa's).

So that's what I wrote about. It wasn't Paris.

"That was, um, a very detailed travelogue, Anvi," Ms. Puri was saying. She had come over to listen to our group for a few minutes. "Thank you for sharing. Now, who is next?"

To my astonishment, Lakshmi raised her hand.

"Yes, please, Lakshmi." Ms. Puri nodded. "We would love to hear what you have to say."

Lakshmi cleared her throat. "Summer Holiday," she announced. "By Lakshmi."

Anvi snickered, but Ms. Puri glared at her and she quieted down.

And then Lakshmi told the most amazing story about going deep into the jungle and coming face to face with this enormous mother tiger who had five tiger cubs trailing behind her. And the mother got shot by this evil poacher. She was lying on her side and bleeding and she would have bled to death if Lakshmi hadn't ripped her *dupatta* into strips and wrapped the strips tightly around the mother tiger's ribs to hold them together. By then, night was falling. The tiger cubs were mewing with hunger. Lakshmi knew she had to build a fire or they would all be eaten by the king cobras hiding in the brush, and so she began rubbing two sticks together, trying to start a fire. She could hear the rustle of the snakes creeping closer. And then, just when she saw a spark of fire, fat raindrops started falling. . . .

"This is stupid!" It was Anvi. "We were *supposed* to write

a *true* story about our *own* summer vacation!" She looked at Ms. Puri. "*Her* story is made up. It's not—"

Ms. Puri interrupted her. "Hmm, I don't recall specifying that this exercise was in autobiographical, narrative-style nonfiction only."

Then she turned to Lakshmi. She had her lips pressed together tightly, like she was trying not to smile. "Still, we weren't expecting quite such a tall tale, Lakshmi."

Lakshmi lowered her head, so we could only see the part in her hair.

"Well, *I* thought it was great!" said Dhruv Gupta.

I bent down to check on Lakshmi. Her head tilted slightly toward me as she grinned at the floor.

Things were definitely harder on Meher. She never talked, never raised her hand in class. Sometimes Ms. Puri would call on her anyway and she would just sit there, staring at the floor, till Ms. Puri moved on to someone else. Maybe it was because Meher's English—especially compared to Lakshmi's—was pretty bad. But she never spoke up in Hindi class, either.

So maybe Anvi was right, and Meher was just plain stupid? I didn't really know. But I think Meher simply didn't know what to say most of the time.

Once, when we were doing a unit on marine habitats, Ms. Puri asked us to describe the sounds and sights of the ocean. Everyone got all excited, raising their hands. Of course, I had tons to say because I've spent so much time at Nana and Grandpa's on Cape Cod. And Anvi was psyched because she had been to Miami and the Maldives and Saint-Tropez and a bunch of beaches in Thailand. Even Lakshmi had seen the ocean down south. Everybody else had at least been to Goa. So kids were yelling stuff out like "The waves go crash!" or "There are seagulls and peanut *chaat*!" or "We made a huge sand castle!" Ms. Puri was very busy writing all our ideas down on the blackboard.

Then Ms. Puri called on Meher—I think she was trying to be inclusive—but Meher just sat there, looking at the floor. She didn't make a peep.

I didn't think much of it but later, after school, Lakshmi brought it up. "I don't know why she call on Meher," Lakshmi said. Her voice was tight with anger. "Meher never see ocean!" Lakshmi waved a hand, gesturing at the buildings surrounding the park. "She never go outside this place. She know only this! Only this!"

Lakshmi dropped her hand and her shoulders sagged. Her voice grew quiet. "How can she talk about ocean when she never leave this place?"

Chapter 14

I was still hanging out with Anvi and Prisha and their group, but I had yet to go over to anybody's house. When Anvi asked me about it—her mom had texted another invitation to my mom—I changed the subject.

Then Anvi's birthday came. It was going to be the biggest bash ever, she said. It was going to be *awesome*. And it was going to be at her parents' farmhouse in Chattarpur. I *had* to come.

There's a rule at Premium Academy: If you hand out birthday invitations at school, you have to bring one for everyone in the class. You can't leave anyone out.

One Wednesday afternoon, Anvi's driver and *didi* showed up at school with two enormous cardboard boxes full of invitations. Each invitation was in its own thin sparkly box, about the size of an iPad. You opened the box and a pop song blared out. I couldn't understand the song—it was in

Hindi—but Anvi made sure that everyone knew her dad had commissioned it from some famous Bollywood singer-songwriter in Bombay. The song was about her.

Ms. Puri made Anvi wait till the end of school to hand out the invitations. When the final bell rang, all the girls swarmed Anvi and the two boxes. Anvi called out names and then handed each girl an invitation, one by one. The girls lifted the box tops and squealed when the music played.

When she got to me, Anvi handed over my invitation with a special, secretive smile. I opened the box. There was a little card tucked inside. It was candy pink and heart-shaped. It looked just like a valentine. I turned it over and there, scribbled in gold metallic marker, were the following words:
ANVI + CHLOE = BFF!

Best friends forever.

I felt my face flush.

It was like that moment when Charlie Bucket peels off the wrapper of the Whipple-Scrumptious Fudgemallow Delight and he finds Willy Wonka's last golden ticket inside. Anvi Saxena wanted to be best friends with me—with Charlie-Bucket-of-a-*me*!

I glanced up at Anvi, who was still busy handing out invitations. Her long arms reached down into the cardboard boxes. Her delicate fingers handed out the sparkly invitations. Her black hair shone in the fluorescent light of the classroom. She looked like a movie star. She looked perfect.

Anvi was reaching the bottom of the first box. She frowned as she pulled out two invitations and held them for a moment, one in each hand, as if she were weighing them. Then she looked across the classroom. Lakshmi and Meher were by the windows, watching the rest of us. Lakshmi was leaning back against the wall, her arms crossed over her chest. She and Meher weren't talking. They were just standing there, watching.

Anvi cleared her throat. "Well, are you going to take them?" she said.

Neither girl budged.

"Meher!" Anvi commanded.

Lakshmi gave Meher a little nudge and the mousy girl trudged up to Anvi. She held out her hand, her eyes still on the ground.

Anvi took her time. She swung her long hair so that it all cascaded over one shoulder. Finally she placed the invitation in Meher's hand. Meher slunk back to the window, the invitation at her side.

"Now *you*?" Anvi said, eyebrows arched.

Lakshmi strode across the room. Her black eyes blazed straight into Anvi's. She put out her hand, but Anvi held the invitation tight to her chest for a moment.

Then she turned to me. "I don't know why we waste our money on these invitations for them," she said. "It's not like they'll come. . . ."

I flinched. I couldn't look at Lakshmi, who was standing in front of Anvi, her hand still extended, palm up.

Everyone was staring at the two girls now. It was a standoff.

Where, oh where, was Ms. Puri? I glanced frantically around the room, but I didn't see her. She must have stepped out for a moment. Why wasn't she there?

Right then, a pack of boys came tumbling back into the classroom. They had been in the bathroom, changing into uniforms for after-school cricket club.

"What's the matter, Anvi?" Dhruv snorted. "Your invitations too precious to give away?"

Anvi glared at Dhruv. Then, rather than placing the invitation in Lakshmi's hand, she tossed it toward her. The invitation bounced off Lakshmi's chest and landed on the floor.

Everyone stared. They were expecting Lakshmi to bend over and pick up the invitation. But Lakshmi just looked down at the envelope for a moment. Then she took one giant step. Her oversized school shoe landed on top of the sparkly box. A strangled noise came out of it and then stopped. The classroom was silent.

Anvi stood there, openmouthed, too shocked to speak.

Lakshmi kept walking, right out of the classroom. She didn't look back, not even when Dhruv and the other boys erupted into hoots of laughter. She simply strode away, her long black braids swishing behind her.

We were sitting on the seesaw in the park later that afternoon. It was so hot I could feel the seesaw's metal seat burning through my nylon shorts.

"Was Anvi right?" I said.

"Huh?" said Lakshmi.

"About her party. You'd never go?"

Lakshmi snorted. "No."

"Why not?"

Lakshmi gave me a hard look.

"Anvi *tried* to give you an invitation," I said. I shifted my bum on the burning seat. "I was there."

Rather than answering me, Lakshmi stuck her fingers in the corners of her mouth and let out a whistle. Kali came trotting out of the bushes. Lakshmi leaned down and muttered something to the dog as she stroked her scarred head.

I tried again later. We were under the AC in Mom's office. I was teaching Lakshmi Uno.

"You sure you won't come to Anvi's party?"

Lakshmi didn't look up from her cards.

"No," she said.

"How come?" I said. "It would be more fun with you there. . . ."

Finally Lakshmi looked up at me. She tilted her head to one side as she spoke. "You not talk with me at party, Chloe," she said.

I fiddled with my cards, closing my hand, then fanning it back out again. I could feel my face getting hot.

"We not school friends," Lakshmi continued. Her voice was gentle but firm, matter of fact. It was like she wanted to reassure me that things were all right—that it was okay that we didn't hang out at school, that we didn't act like friends when Anvi and Prisha were around. We were friends in secret. And that was okay with her.

"Well, you didn't have to step on the invitation," I said. I placed a red five on the discard pile. "You could have just—I dunno—walked around it. Or maybe picked it up and said, like, 'I'm so sorry, but I can't make it that day,' or something."

Lakshmi played a red seven. "But this make more—what you say?" She grinned mischievously. "This make more splash?"

I played a red skip, a blue skip, and a blue seven.

"Uno!" Lakshmi yelled. She pointed at the one remaining card in my hand.

"Shit!" I said. Then I clamped my free hand over my mouth. "Oops, pretend you didn't hear that. You're not supposed to say that, okay?"

"Shit, shit, shit!" Lakshmi echoed. "Now you draw two!" She watched gleefully as I picked up two cards.

"I beating you, Chloe," Lakshmi crowed. "This new game for me, but I know more than you already."

After Lakshmi left, I went to the kitchen to grab a snack. Anna was there, peeling an orange. I reached into the cupboard for a packet of Delishus biscuits. (And no, they're not all that delicious.)

"She doesn't have a car, you know," Anna said.

"What?"

Anna stopped peeling the orange for a second and looked

at me. "Lakshmi," she said. "She doesn't have a car. And she probably doesn't have the right clothes. Or money for a present. So how do you expect her to go to some stupid birthday party?"

"Were you eavesdropping on me and my friend?" I said.

Anna turned back to her peeling. "I just think you should realize," she said, "that life might be a little more complicated for Lakshmi."

"And I think you should realize"—I was shouting now—"that you should mind your own business!"

I slammed the cupboard and stormed out of the kitchen, a fat stack of cookies in my hand.

Chapter 15

A uniformed guard pulled open the iron gate to Anvi Saxena's house and Vijay drove the minivan up the long, topiary-lined driveway, coming to a stop under the columned portico where two gold Porsches and a silver Rolls-Royce gleamed like family trophies to welcome us.

"Good grief," Mom muttered.

Since Mom had been killing herself on some big story for weeks, I was surprised when she offered to take me to Anvi's party. She even blow-dried her hair and put on some mascara for the occasion. As for me, I was wearing jeggings and my favorite sparkly tank top. I had even convinced Mom to paint my fingernails pink.

"Just for the party," Mom warned as she blew on my wet polish. "We'll take it off as soon as we get home."

We walked up the wide marble steps, past two enormous lion sculptures, but before we could reach the front door, a man in a dove-gray uniform darted forward and ushered us back down the steps, toward the side of the house, where a massive tunnel of pink and silver balloons stretched into the mansion's back lawns. Dance music pounded in the distance.

"Jeez," Mom said, looking up. "There must be hundreds of balloons here just for this one day. What a waste. Imagine the impact on the environment if every—"

"Mom!"

"Sorry, sorry!" Mom said, clamping a hand over her mouth. She gave me a little nudge. "I'll try to behave, okay?"

I tugged at the stretchy headband I was wearing. My hair had grown out a lot since the Magic Marker incident, but little bits sometimes stuck out at funny angles.

"You look great, sweetie," Mom said.

"You're my mom," I said flatly. "You're supposed to say that."

Still, my heart rose when we stepped out of the balloon tunnel and the vast green lawns of the Saxena estate spread out before us.

"Jeez," Mom said again. "Shreya said it would be big, but I wasn't expecting a country club."

To our left, an immense swimming pool, surrounded by tables and sun loungers, sparkled under the midday sun. Behind it was a tennis court. An enormous lawn stretched along the back of the property, a cell phone tower looming over it like an alien spaceship. Soccer goals had been set up at either end of the lawn, and even though it was boiling, some boys from my class had started a game.

As we stood there, slightly dazzled, a skinny lady in an off-the-shoulder top and tight white jeans teetered toward us. She was wearing high heels, and with each step, they sank a bit into the soft grass, making her wobble from side to side. She was trailed by a tall, uniformed man wearing mirrored sunglasses. He looked a lot like the guy I had seen dropping Anvi off at school, except this one had a thin black mustache and a tattoo across one bulging bicep—a dagger with a curved tip. I glanced around. That's when I realized they were positioned all along the perimeter of the Saxena property: guys in identical dark gray uniforms and mirrored sunglasses. Each one held a walkie-talkie.

They were security guards.

"Welcome! Welcome!" The wobbling woman had finally reached us. She gave my mom a big, fake smile and my mom gave her a big, fake smile back.

"You must be Klow-ay! Anvi told me about you! We're sooo happy you could make it to her little party!"

Anvi's mom spoke in exclamations and when she leaned down to squeeze my cheek with her long purple fingernails, her face didn't look quite so pretty. Up close, I could see that her makeup had caked a bit around her mouth and eyes. The eyes themselves were a weird color, kind of blotchy green. Her hair was lighter than most Indian hair, too—blondish brown instead of black. It hung in long, loose curls over her shoulders and down her back. I'm no hair expert, but even I could tell a lot of work had gone into that hair.

I found myself fidgeting with my headband again.

"Are you from Manhattan?" Anvi's mom was exclaiming to my mom.

"No," Mom said. "Actually, we're from Massachu—"

"We have a penthouse in Manhattan! Fifty-Seventh and Lexington! Love the shopping! Sooo much better than Delhi! But at least we have Dubai!"

Mom elbowed me and I held my gift up. "Thank you for inviting me, Mrs. Saxena," I said.

Anvi's mom seemed confused by both my declaration and the presentation of the gift—two Roald Dahl paperbacks, which Mom had wrapped in brown paper that I had potato-printed that morning. She waved at a servant to come take the parcel from my hands. Then, before we could say another word, she had lurched off, chasing down a caterer with a silver tray while the tattooed bodyguard followed.

Abandoned, Mom and I stood there for a moment, surveying the scene. The party was already in full swing. There was an enormous pink bouncy castle set up in one corner of the lawn, as well as a bunch of other amusement-park-style rides: a rocking ship, spinning teacups, and a mini train for the littler kids. Back by the soccer field, a zip line had been strung from one end of the lawn to the other, and kids were already lined up, waiting to be harnessed for a ride. There was a huge inflatable ball that two kids could be strapped into and then rolled around in. There was also a mechanical bull. Closer to us, an oversized trampoline was outfitted with a bungee cord so that kids could jump as high as the third-floor balconies of the Saxenas' marble mansion.

Uniformed staff members were scurrying around, strapping kids into the various contraptions. Most kids had an ayah trailing behind them, too. There were hardly any parents, though—just a couple of moms seated at a round table by the pool, chatting. They had big sunglasses on, and big bags in their laps. Each one clutched an iPhone, which she tapped every couple of minutes.

"I'm gonna case the joint, maybe find a ladies' room," Mom said. "You don't hear from me in an hour, you call the cops, okay?" She jerked her thumb over her shoulder, toward the house. "I could get lost in that marble quarry." She leaned down and kissed me on the head. "Have fun, sweetie." Then she set off toward the house, her long cotton skirt swaying as her flip-flops flapped against the grass.

I gave an involuntary shudder. I love my mom and I didn't want her to be like those other moms—really, I didn't—but did she have to be so, so . . . *not* like them?

Scanning the crowd, I spotted Anvi and Prisha toward the back, by the zip line. There was a fashion-show runway set up and they were strutting down it, striking poses and then collapsing against each other in hysterics.

A sudden attack of shyness hit me.

Instead of joining them, I slunk over to the crafts area, where a bunch of bored-looking helpers were slumped behind a long row of activity tables: BeDazzle your own T-shirt, get your own hair extensions, make your own tiara. I paused in front of the nail stall, where bottles of polish were stacked in pyramids. There had to be at least fifty different shades.

"You want?" A young Thai-looking woman pointed at her

own nails, which were decorated with skulls-and-roses decals.

I shook my head. Mom would kill me.

"No thanks," I said.

She shrugged and went back to texting.

I was gluing yellow feathers onto a mask when the MC turned on his microphone and started trying to corral the kids into party games.

"Let's get ready to PAR-TEEEY!" he yelled into the mike.

Even though it was blazingly hot, he wore a shiny black suit and a sparkly silver tie. Sweat streamed down his temples.

"It's Princess Anvi's birthday, and we're going to have MAXIMUM FUN!"

He had one of those really fake American accents. He was yelling so loud, I could feel the table under my mask vibrate.

"Don't you want to play, honey?"

Mom was standing at my elbow.

"I like your mask," she said.

I squinted up at her. Then I shrugged. "I'm not really in the mood," I said.

"But you love party games," Mom persisted. "Back home, you always wanted to play."

"That was home," I said.

Mom sat down in the chair next to mine. "You okay?"

I kept gluing. We had been at the party for twenty minutes already and Anvi hadn't even come over to say hi. I didn't understand. She gave me the BFF card, right? Maybe she had already changed her mind. Maybe she didn't want to be friends with me after all. Maybe I was too boring. Maybe I was like that petal-pink backpack and she was already . . .

"Yo, everybody! Come on up for tug-of-war! Tug-of-war, everybody! Give it on up for ANVI!" the MC yelled in the background.

"Why don't you give it a try, Chloe?" Mom said. "Just play one game, and then . . ." She gave me a nudge. "And then we can get out of here, okay? Maybe stop at the bookstore on the way home?"

I didn't say anything.

Mom stood up. "I think you might regret it if you don't even try. . . ."

I sighed. I knew my mom; she was not going to give up without a fight. "Okay, okay," I grumbled. "I'll play one stupid game."

The next time I saw Mom it was three hours and several dozen rounds of freeze dance later. I was huddled with Anvi and Prisha at the body-painting table when Mom stomped up, her face cloudy.

"Oh, you must be Anvi! We haven't met! I'm Chloe's mom!" Mom said. She was talking fast. Her voice was fake cheery.

Anvi stared at her without saying anything.

"Well!" Mom said, turning to me. "You ready to go, sweetie? I think we better get back to Dad and Lucy. And I'm sure you have homework to do." She glanced around at all the girls at the table and lowered her voice. "I'm sure you *all* have homework to do," she said.

The girls stared back at her, their expressions blank.

"I'll be in the car, Chloe," she said, then turned and flip-flopped toward the balloon tunnel.

"Why do you have to be such a downer, Mom?" I said.

We were stuck in a line of cars trying to get out of the farmhouse compound and onto the ring road toward home.

Mom didn't answer.

"Mom?" I said. I knew I was pushing it, but I couldn't stop myself.

"Oh, *I'm* the downer?" Mom said. "Wasn't *I* the one who had to push *you* into joining the party games? And let's review what happened next, shall we? Hmm, I sat for three hours in the blazing sun, being force-fed chicken chunks while listening to those . . . to those women—who seem to do nothing with their lives but get their hair done—complain about their maids ironing their lingerie the wrong way." She paused to take a breath. "I would actually argue, Chloe, that I was rather supportive today."

The car was silent for a few moments.

"Did you like the food?" I was backpedaling, trying to make peace.

"Oh, Chloe," Mom said. She paused for a moment. "The

food was delicious, sweetie. But it was so . . . it was so over the top. I mean, *all* that food. Did we need even a quarter of it?"

I looked out the window. She was right, of course. There had been way too much food. A catered buffet the length of an Olympic-sized pool spread along one side of the garden with dish after dish of Indian kiddie favorites: *chaat* and *kati* rolls, *dosas, chhole bhature,* and *rajma chawal.* There was a pasta station and a pizza station. There were custom-made quesadillas, burritos, and shawarmas. Mongolian barbecue. Crepes. There was a make-your-own salad bar and a sandwich table. There were chicken hot dogs and chicken burgers served with fries. And piles of steaming naan, served piping hot from two tandoor ovens.

The dessert buffet was over by the tennis court: oven-fresh cookies and made-to-order waffles, a chocolate fountain and ice cream sundaes. There was a candy bar with a dozen glass canisters full of sour bombs, toffees, and chocolates. They even had cellophane bags in case you wanted your candies to go. On a separate, round table, surrounded by white lilies, was the cake, a standing replica of Anvi herself dressed in a silver miniskirt made of sugar crystals that sparkled in the sun. She was holding a mobile phone and a handbag made of marzipan. ("It's a Kelly," Anvi whispered to me. When she saw my blank look, she rolled her eyes. "The bag! It's a Kelly. You know, Hermès? I got a real one as a present.") When the MC put on a hip-hop remix of "Happy Birthday," actual fireworks went off—even though it was daytime.

I sighed.

"Sure, you're right, Mom. But it was a party, you know? I mean, that's what people *do* here."

Mom took a deep breath. "Chloe," she finally said. She was speaking slowly, enunciating her words. "You need to understand something. You need to believe me when I tell you that when your father and I decided to send you to an Indian school, we never expected that you and your sister would be exposed to this kind of opulence, this kind of privilege. . . ."

"Then why did you, Mom? I mean, it's like I can't win! You want me to go to an Indian school and so I do. But then, when I finally make some friends and get invited to the birthday party of the most popular girl in class and do what *you* say and play the games and try to fit in, then you tell me it's no good. I just don't get it. *What do you want me to do?*"

I was crying now. Hot tears were streaming down my cheeks.

"Oh, sweetie," Mom said. She reached over and took my hand. "I know you're trying. I know it isn't easy."

I pulled my hand away. "No," I said. "You *don't* know." I was crying harder. "You don't. . . ."

"Chloe . . ."

Vijay had reached down and now, without a word, was handing a box of tissues through the gap between the front seats. He had seen scenes like this before.

"Thank you, Vijay." Mom pulled out a tissue and handed it to me. I blew.

"You might not understand how valuable this experience is right now. But later, when you look back on your childhood, you'll be so proud of this time. It will have taught you so much. . . ."

"Not everything has to be a lesson, Mom," I said. "Why can't some things just be, just be . . . fun?"

Mom was silent for a moment. She looked out the window. Then, rather than speaking, she pointed. We were stopped at the same red light by the market between home and school. As we idled, some kids scampered up a pile of garbage. They were laughing and pointing. I looked up to see half a dozen kites swooping and darting, lunging at each other in the bright blue sky.

"It looks like *they're* having fun," Mom said. She closed her eyes and rubbed her thumbs in circles against her temples. "You know, you don't need a bungee cord and a zip line—"

"I know, Mom," I interrupted.

One of the kites swooped too low and landed in some electrical wires by the side of the road. Two boys sprinted over, pushing and shoving, each trying to be the first to climb up a concrete pillar and free the kite from the twisted knot of wires.

The light turned green. Vijay stepped on the gas and the boys disappeared behind us.

Mom opened her eyes again. She looked over at me. "I suppose . . . ," she began. "I suppose I'm concerned about you being overly influenced by all the privilege around you. I don't want you to . . . to change."

"If you don't want me to change, then why did you bring me here in the first place?" I said.

Mom thought before she spoke. "So that . . . well . . .

that . . . well, we—your father and I—we wanted you and Anna and Lucy to see that every place isn't just like Boston. That there's a strange and fascinating world out there . . ."

"Where some kids have bungee cord birthdays and some kids play on piles of garbage," I said.

Mom smiled a little. "Yeah," she said.

Vijay was pulling the car to a stop in front of our house. He turned the motor off. It was silent for a moment. I picked up the party favor—a large box wrapped in sparkly pink paper with a silver bow. I knew with complete certainty that it would be a much fancier, pricier gift than the two paperbacks I had given Anvi. I knew that fact shouldn't matter to me. But it did.

Chapter 16

I couldn't sleep that night. Maybe it was all the candy and Sprite at the party. Maybe it was the fight with Mom in the car afterward.

I got out of bed. The house was quiet and dark. I snuck into Mom's office. Her laptop was humming on her desk. I flipped it open and a Word document popped up:

There's No Place Like No Home
Slum Clearances Leave Delhi's Poor Desperate and Homeless

It had to be the feature story that Mom had been slaving over these past couple of weeks. My eyes scanned the first paragraph:

Ashok Kumar, 37, has no running water or electricity in the 500-square-foot one-room brick dwelling he shares with his wife and two daughters, but it's eviction that he worries about. He is one of Delhi's estimated 5 million unauthorized settlers . . .

I clicked on another tab and Mom's Gmail account popped up. I placed my fingers on the keys, took a deep breath, and started typing.

> To: Katie Standish
> Subject: Hi!
>
> Dear Katie,
> I miss you a lot. Things are pretty good here, but they're also really different than back home. I went to a birthday party today and they had this huge zip line and a mechanical bull! It was fun but also kind of weird.
>   I have this friend Lakshmi. She's Indian, with two long braids all the way down to her waist. She's not really like the other girls at school. And then I have this other friend called Anvi. She's the one who had the birthday party. And Lakshmi didn't come to the party. I'm not even really friends with her at school.

I'm not very good at typing, so that's as far as I got. It wasn't just the typing, actually. It's that I didn't know how to explain what I wanted to say. I mean, how could I describe the differences between Anvi and Lakshmi and why we didn't all hang out together? If I didn't really get it, how could I explain it to Katie? And why would she care anyway? There weren't these same kind of differences back in Boston. At least, not in our school. Or maybe I hadn't noticed them there, I guess. I was on my own in figuring this situation out.

I clicked on discard draft. Then I closed the computer and went back to bed.

Part Three

THE MISFITS

Chapter 17

Annual Day was coming. The excitement had been building for weeks. There would be a big show to celebrate the
school's birthday. All the parents were invited. It would happen at night, under the stage lights. Each class would get
costumes and perform a special dance routine. The evening
would culminate (which means *wrap it up already!*) with the
handing out of special academic awards.

Honestly, since we don't have anything like Annual Day
back home, I didn't understand what all the fuss was about.
But I could tell it was a big deal here. Even Ms. Puri—who
is usually pretty chill about this kind of stuff—was telling us
to get our hair cut.

The problem that Annual Day raised for me was the
dancing. I stink at it.

Back in Boston, we had no separate dance class—just a
couple of square-dancing lessons during third-grade gym—

but at Premium Academy, dancing was an obsession. We had dance class several times a week. And now, with Annual Day coming up, we had hours and hours of dance practice every day.

For the Indian kids, this was great. Indian kids love to dance. They do it all the time at huge family functions, like weddings that last for days. And they watch endless Bollywood movies where the actors break into huge, flashy dance numbers. The kids in my class never get self-conscious and never seem to worry about how silly they might look with their hands pumping up and down in the air. They just do it. And they're good, too. Really good. All the girls in my class know how to shimmy their shoulders and wiggle their hips. They can twist their wrists and tap their feet and wiggle their butts all at the same time. Me? I only dance at home with the door to my room shut, earbuds stuck in my ears so that no one else will know what I'm up to. And preferably with the lights off.

So for me, this whole Annual Day extravaganza was a source of stress. The dance routine—with its complicated choreography and fancy footwork—was way too hard. Just getting to the right spot on the stage at the right time was a major challenge.

As a result, Mr. Bhatnagar, the dance instructor, had stuck me in the very back, half-hidden by some large potted palm trees. I was supposed to stand there for most of the routine and wave my arms over my head to "add some very nice texture," as Mr. Bhatnagar put it. Lakshmi and Meher were stuck back there with me, too. But at the very end of the routine, for the grand finale, the three of us were supposed to skip forward—carefully avoiding three pyramids of boys and two spinning girls—to join a line of dancing girls, which would then snake out to the exit. The tricky part for me was catching the cue. All the Hindi lyrics sounded the same, so I kept missing the moment when I had to start my skip—and I was leading Lakshmi and Meher, who were supposed to stay tucked behind me.

At least I wasn't the only person struggling with the finale. The real problem was the spins. Mr. Bhatnagar insisted that two girls in the front and center had to perform five full spins in perfect synchronicity, which means at exactly the same time. Even the very best dancers in the class—Anvi and Prisha—couldn't get the spins right. They tried and tried, but there were too many spins. They'd get dizzy and stumble out of position or be unable to synchronize. One always seemed to finish before the other. So we practiced and practiced in the playground during recess—Anvi and Prisha doing the spins while I counted.

But it wasn't happening; the spins were too hard.

Still, Mr. Bhatnagar wouldn't give up.

Then things really fell apart. It happened on a Friday afternoon, the week before Annual Day. We had been rehearsing the finale for an hour already. Things were *not* going well.

Mr. Bhatnagar paced across the front of the stage, shaking his bald head in frustration.

"Again! Again! A-one-two-three-four . . ." He clapped his

hands and tinny music blared from the speakers. It was our ninth run-through.

I stood in my spot in the back beside the potted palm trees, waving my hands in the air, but my mind had drifted to Boston, where last year I had starred in *Christina and the Moonbeam Pullers,* a play written by Mrs. Rose, the elementary-school drama teacher. As Christina, I got to wear my pajamas onstage and sing a solo while swinging on a real swing set up on . . .

Lakshmi poked me, so I started skipping forward, but I was on autopilot. My mind was still in Boston, where, at the end of the play, the whole audience had stood up and given me a standing ovation. I could see my parents in the front row. . . .

"Chloe!" Lakshmi yelped. "Watch out!"

I snapped to, just in time to see Anvi spinning toward me. She was twirling so fast, her long black hair fanned out around her like a parasol. I tried to duck out of the way, but it was too late.

POW!

Anvi crashed into me and we both toppled to the floor. We lay there in two heaps, stunned for a moment.

"Bas! Bas!" Mr. Bhatnagar bellowed.

The music screeched to a halt.

The boys scrambled out of their pyramids. They stood in one large clump, laughing and pointing.

I glanced around. Everyone was laughing.

I could feel my cheeks heating up and turning red.

"Look, she is red like *rajma*!" Dhruv Gupta cackled. "We should not call her Chhole! We should call her Rajma only!"

Some boys hooted.

"*Bas!*" Mr. Bhatnagar barked. "Take your places!"

I picked myself up off the floor. "Anvi? Anvi, are you okay?"

But Anvi turned her head away, pretending not to hear.

Prisha helped Anvi up. Wrapping her arm around Anvi's shoulders, she guided her back to their spot in center stage and whispered something in Anvi's ear.

I slunk back to my spot in the back row.

"You okay, Chloe?" Lakshmi whispered.

I shook my head, blinking back tears.

Mr. Bhatnagar was standing at the front of the stage now, his shoulders slumped. He had taken off his glasses and was massaging his temples with his fat, stubby fingers.

Maybe the pressure was getting to him. Annual Day was next week. He had made us practice our dance over and over, but we just couldn't get that last bit of the ending right. (If someone had asked me, it was because those five spins were too tough. But no one *had* asked me. And Anvi would never admit to anyone—even herself—that she couldn't do them. She was Anvi Saxena; she *needed* to be the star of the show.)

When he finally spoke, Mr. Bhatnagar was still staring at the floor and shaking his head slowly. His voice was low and tired. From my spot in the back, I had to strain to hear him.

"Annual Day is next Wednesday night," he said. "We have very less time. The finale must be tip-top."

He put his glasses back on, then took a deep breath and looked up at us. He shrugged his shoulders as if he were apologizing.

"You give me no choice, you see. . . ."

The girls glanced at each other, their eyebrows raised.

Mr. Bhatnagar cleared his throat before he spoke again. "There will be one competition. The two girls who perform five full spins in a row at the same time and in very best fashion will get top marks for the same." He held five fat fingers up for emphasis. "Five spins. No falling. No stepping out of position. Perfect timing. Perfectly together." He dropped his hand back to his side. "Pick your partner with utmost care. And this weekend, maximum practice. The competition will take place on Monday."

With that, he turned and walked out of the room.

There was a moment of stunned silence.

"But . . ." I heard Prisha Kapoor say. She still had her arm around Anvi's shoulders. "But . . . but . . . that's supposed to be us. We're supposed to be doing the spins. That's the routine!"

Anvi shook herself from Prisha's grasp. She spun around to glare at me, her eyes narrowed, her hands clenched into fists. "It's because of Chloe!" she hissed. "She knocked me over. And now we all have to go through these stupid tryouts! We don't have time for this! It's going to ruin our performance!"

"But I . . . ," I said. "But I was doing the right thing. I was in the right spot. *You* were the one who crashed into *me*!"

"You *always* ruin *everything*!" Anvi's eyes flicked from me to Lakshmi, who was still standing next to me at the back of the stage. "You and your *special* friend," she hissed.

Anvi spun on her heels, her long black hair flying out behind her. As she strode off the stage, I could just catch what she said to Prisha: "Mama will get Shiamak. We'll practice in my home dance studio all weekend. I know I'm the best dancer in class. We're sure to be picked!"

Chapter 18

I spread the contents of my jewelry box on the bedspread and then flopped down on my tummy, thinking we could paw through it and try on junk rings, but Lakshmi only hovered in the doorway, surveying the scene.

I am not a tidy person. Saturdays are particularly bad for me because I have a pact with Dechen: she won't enter my room till late afternoon. Which means that by five o'clock on Saturday, the place is a biohazard.

My bed was a mess. There were piles of clothes in the corner of the room and books scattered across the rug. My trunk was half-open, scarves and hats and various bags spilling out. Some outgrown toys were pushed under the bed. A half-finished jigsaw puzzle of the Taj Mahal covered one corner of the floor. I'd been working on it for a couple of days, so pieces were littered about. A partially eaten peanut butter sandwich sat on the night table.

"Sorry for the mess," I said.

Lakshmi shrugged and walked over to the bookcase. She leaned forward and picked up an old Barbie from the clutter on the top shelf. It was an American Barbie with blond hair, pink skin, arched feet, and big boobs. It was also butt naked. (Indian Barbies have white plastic granny panties built in.)

Lakshmi turned the Barbie around, inspecting it carefully. She touched the Barbie's hair.

"You want it?" I said. "You can have it." I hadn't played with that Barbie in years. I don't even know why Mom had brought it from Boston, especially since she herself hates Barbies. You do *not* want to get her started on that subject.

Lakshmi stroked the Barbie's hair for a few minutes. Then she walked over to me—still lying on the bed—and reached out to touch my hair. It felt a little weird.

"Gold," she said.

"Um, no, not gold," I replied, ducking my head out of her reach. "It's blond. My hair is blond."

"So pretty," Lakshmi said. "You hair so pretty."

I gave her a funny look. "I wish it were dark, like yours," I said.

Lakshmi shook her head. "Everyone in America have fair hair," she said.

"Um, no," I corrected her. "No, they don't. What about Anna? She's American and her hair's practically black."

Lakshmi was silent for a moment, still staring at the Barbie. "She look like Katrina Kaif," she said. "But she . . ." She hesitated, pursing her lips together. "But blond. She blond."

"Katrina Kaif?" I said. "Who's that?"

Lakshmi's eyebrows practically disappeared into her

hairline. "Who Katrina Kaif?" she exclaimed. "She megastar. She *Ek Tha Tiger*. She *Tees Maar Khan*. . . ."

When I shrugged, Lakshmi leapt up onto my bed. With one hard push, she shoved me to the floor.

"Hey . . ."

But Lakshmi was already on her knees on my bed. She was pulling the top sheet up around her chest. She started pumping her chest up and back, flinging her schoolgirl braids from side to side. She closed her eyes, lifted her chin, and started to sing: "I know you want it but you're never going to get it, *tere haath kabhi na aani*. . . ."

Then she threw the sheet down and sprang off the bed. She started sashaying up and down the room, shaking her hips from side to side and waving her hands above her head. Puzzle pieces went flying.

"My name is Sheila, Sheila Ki Jawani! I'm too sexy for you. . . ."

I sat on the floor, staring up at her.

She was transformed. She was amazing.

After a good five minutes of singing, clapping, shoulder shimmying, and hip gyrating, Lakshmi finally collapsed on her back on the bed. I could see her chest heaving through her kurta.

"Oh my God," I said. "That was . . . that was brilliant."

Lakshmi grinned up at the ceiling.

"I didn't know you could dance like that. You never dance like that in school."

Lakshmi shrugged.

"How'd you learn?"

"My cousin brother have Tata Sky high-definition TV." She was still breathing hard.

"Wow," I said. "Does he get a lot of movies? I mean, do you know how to do a lot of dances?"

Instead of answering, Lakshmi pulled herself off the bed again, crouched down on the floor, then popped back up, doing a full split in the air. She landed and went straight into a spin, ending with a fist pump.

I stared at her, my mouth open. "That would be a 'yes,'" I said.

Lakshmi nodded. "I do all dance: Madhuri Dixit, Sridevi, Meenakshi Sheshadri—"

I cut off her list of Hindi movie stars. "So maybe you could teach me?" I said. "I mean, you could help me with the dance? The Annual Day dance?"

Lakshmi grinned. "Piece of . . . what you say? Biscuit?"

"Cake," I said. "Piece of cake."

Except it wasn't.

See, what *I* had meant was that Lakshmi could help me with that tricky little bit of the finale—the part where she and Meher and I were supposed to skip forward to join the line of dancing girls snaking out to the exit. I figured it would take fifteen minutes of rehearsing, tops. But what *Lakshmi* wanted to work on was the spins.

"No way," I said, shaking my head. "There is no way that I could ever do those spins. No way. No how. Never."

But Lakshmi insisted. She blocked the door with her little stick body and crossed her arms over her chest. She wasn't going to let me out of the room (*my* room!) till I at least gave it a shot.

I shook my head again. "There's no point, Lakshmi. I can't do them."

"If there no point, it not hurt to try, *na?*" she said.

"All right, all right," I groaned. "I'll give you fifteen minutes to teach me how to do five spins. Then we're having lunch."

Lakshmi grinned. "Deal!"

One hour later, she was still drilling me. She was a tough teacher, but a good one, showing me how to turn on the ball of my left foot, keeping my right foot close so that I wouldn't fall out of position, and how to pick a spot on the wall and stare at it so I wouldn't lose my balance. Heading into the next turn, I had to whip my head around and find that same spot again. And again. And again.

"Head up! Chest up! Arm in!" Lakshmi barked.

Dad poked his head into my room. "What's going on in here, girls?" he asked. "Don't you want some lunch? Dechen made grilled cheese."

"Give us a few more minutes, Dad," I said. "Five minutes. We're working on something."

"Okeydokey," he said. "Five more minutes, then time to eat." His head disappeared.

I hit the play button and "Desi Girl"—our Annual Day song—blared out from the tiny speaker on my iPad.

Lakshmi wasn't the only one doing the teaching; I had drummed some phrases into her.

"Take it from the top!" she commanded in a perfect American accent. "A-five, a-six. A-five, six, seven, eight . . ."

Lakshmi spun on the left side . . . I spun on the right . . . one, two, three, four, five . . . we nailed it! We ended at exactly the same time, our arms extended toward the ceiling, our hands twisting in sync to the music.

"Screw the lightbulb! Screw the lightbulb!"

Our hands twisted in the air.

"And freeze!"

We froze, the music stopped, and everything went quiet.

Then I started jumping up and down. "I did it, Lakshmi! I really did it!" I held my fist up at her, chest level, expecting a congratulatory fist bump in return.

"What this?" Lakshmi asked, pointing at my fist.

"It's a fist bump, Lakshmi! C'mon, do it!"

Lakshmi just stood there, her arms glued by her sides.

"You know, it's a sign of friendship, um, like a cooler version of a high five?"

I took her hand and formed it into a fist, then bumped our fists together.

Lakshmi grinned.

I flopped down on the bed. "Oh my God," I said. It was slowly dawning on me. "We could actually do this. We could actually steal the show."

"Steal the show?" Lakshmi echoed. She shook her head. "I never steal, Chloe."

I let out a laugh. "It's just an expression. It means we're going to be the best dancers."

Lakshmi sat down next to me on the edge of the bed. "Better than . . . Anvi?" There was a glint in her black eyes.

Anvi. I was so focused on getting those spins, I had forgotten all about her. What if Lakshmi and I won the dance competition? What if we actually got to do the spins in the finale? Anvi would be beyond furious. She would never forgive me.

I swallowed and then nodded. "Sure," I said. "Even better than Anvi."

We practiced all weekend: Saturday afternoon, Sunday morning, Sunday afternoon.

By Sunday evening, Lakshmi and I could do the spins in perfect synchronicity almost every time we tried them. My shoulders ached. My calves were sore. There was a blister on the bottom of my left foot. But I was happy—as long as I didn't think about Anvi.

Then, as we took a water break on Sunday night, Lakshmi leaned over and picked something up off the floor. It was the pink heart card from Anvi, the one that she had slipped into the birthday party invitation. Before I could grab it, Lakshmi had flipped it over.

"BFF?" she said. "What is BFF?"

"It's stupid," I said.

"Yes, but what does it mean?"

I shrugged and leaned over, pretending to check on my blister. "Best friends forever." I mumbled the words quickly, hoping that she wouldn't hear them and would drop the topic.

But she did hear.

"Best friends forever?" Lakshmi echoed. She looked at me for a moment, her head cocked to one side. "But Anvi doing the spins with Prisha, no?"

I stared down at my toes.

Lakshmi was silent for a moment. Then she gave me a playful shove. "You right, Chloe," she said. "BFF? That *is* stupid."

I still couldn't look up. What was I doing with this spin thing? If I entered the competition with Lakshmi—even if we lost—Anvi might never want to be friends with me again. And then who would I hang out with at Premium Academy? Lakshmi and Meher? Was that what I wanted?

Lakshmi gathered her *dupatta* from the bed. She draped it over her shoulders and then stood up. Without a word, she walked to the door. Right before she opened it, her hand already on the doorknob, she turned back to me. "You know, there no such thing, forever, Chloe," she said. "Nothing is forever."

Then she walked out, closing the door quietly behind her.

Chapter 19

Mondays are the pits. When my alarm goes off at 6:30, I just want to pull the covers up over my head and go back to sleep. Sometimes I do. And then Anna storms into my room, yanks the covers all the way down, and stands there, hands on her uniformed hips, glaring at my curled-up body until I mumble that, yes, I am getting up.

Today she threw my uniform on top of me.

"Hurry up!" she snapped. "It's already 6:56. Vijay and I are leaving for school in nine minutes and you are *not* going to make me late today!"

I groaned, my eyes still closed.

"I mean it, Chloe!" Anna warned. "Mom!" she yelled over her shoulder.

"Okay, okay," I said, pulling myself up to a seated position. I thrust one arm through the sleeve of my uniform, only to find that I was putting it on backward, so I pulled my arm back out.

I was even more tired than usual. Strange dreams had bothered me all night: me dancing with Lakshmi, Lakshmi dancing with Prisha, Mr. Bhatnagar dancing with my mom. All of us spinning, spinning, spinning in endless circles.

"Chloe!" Mom yelled from the kitchen.

"Okay, okay, I'm getting dressed."

First bell rings at 7:25. Last bell rings at 3:15. You do the math.

Yep, that's seven hours and fifty minutes of school. Every. Single. Day.

In Indian school, there is a lot of school.

And boy, do they love testing. We have a test, a quiz, transcription, dictation, or recitation practically every day. First Monday of every month we take a General Knowledge Test, which means I get to make up answers to "universally known" questions like these:

Who was the first Indian bowler to achieve a hat trick in One-Day International matches? (The answer, in case you're wondering: Harbhajan Singh)

Prime Minister Manmohan Singh went to which temple to seek blessings on New Year's Day? (Answer: Siddhivinayak Temple)

Write the full form of the given abbreviation: IAS. (Answer: Indian Administrative Service)

Quizzes are graded. Homework is graded. Classwork is graded. You even get scores for phys ed, music, and dance. Every month, a messenger hand delivers a report card to my parents at home. It has over seventy different grades on it. At the bottom, a bar graph documents my progress. And all these hundreds of grades are accumulated and vetted and tallied and scrutinized and mushed up to determine which ultraspecial half-dozen kids will receive (drumroll, please . . .) the Achievement Awards, which are handed out by the head of the school at the conclusion of the Annual Day performance—in other words, this Wednesday night.

This is not a big deal for me. I've been at the school only a couple of months, so—thank God—I am not eligible for any kind of an award. But it is a *really* big deal for my classmates since they've been working toward these awards for *two years.* The pressure has been ramping up on them since third grade, when all the testing began.

When I got to my classroom (and for the record, we *were* on time), kids were huddled in small groups, their heads close together, whispering. Some had red eyes from crying. Apparently, Mrs. Anand had called a few lucky parents last night to let them know their child had been selected for the Class Five Achievement Award.

It was easy to see who was among the chosen few—those kids were beaming. And I couldn't believe it—one of them was drippy-nosed Dhruv Gupta.

"How about *that,* Chhole?" he crowed as I was hanging my backpack up. "What do you have to say about *that*?"

"About what?" I said, pretending I didn't know what he was talking about.

"About the Achievement Award for yours truly on Wednesday night," Dhruv answered. He gave a little bow.

"You mean achievement in ultra-annoyingness?"

A couple of boys snickered. Dhruv scowled, but before he could say anything, Ms. Puri started clapping her hands to get everybody's attention. She was standing in front of the blackboard, one arm wrapped around Soumya Singh. Poor Soumya—who always wears glasses and a navy-blue head-band and who is really hardworking—was sniffling, her eyes fixed on the floor. She must have been in the running for the award.

"Boys and girls," Ms. Puri said. "Kind thanks for your attention."

The class quieted down.

"The Achievement Award winners have been notified. Let us all extend our heartiest congratulations to these winners for this acknowledgment of their accomplishments."

I felt a jab between my shoulder blades. When I looked around, Dhruv was grinning at me, his eyebrows raised ex-pectantly. I glared and turned back toward the front.

"I want all of you to know"—at this point Ms. Puri gave Soumya's shoulder a tight squeeze—"that each and every one of you is talented in his or her very own way. . . ."

Ms. Puri paused for a moment and that's when Mr. Bhat-nagar burst through the door.

"Ms. Puri?" he said. "A word?"

The two teachers disappeared into the foyer and the classroom erupted into excited chatter. It was as if the Achievement Awards had already been forgotten.

"Anvi, Anvi, did you see?" Prisha was squealing. "It must be about the tryouts! He wants to do them early! He wants to shift the schedule!"

Anvi had been purposefully ignoring me all morning. Now she talked loudly enough that I was sure to overhear. "Hmm," she said. "That *would* make sense. Then we'll have more time to practice our spins with the ensemble this afternoon." She ran her fingers through her hair. "Did I tell you? Papa has taken one extra sponsorship banner, maximum size: 'Congratulations to Anvi, the shining star that spins through our universe. May nothing stand as impossible in your journey to success.'"

"Ooh," said Prisha.

It was at this moment that it dawned on me that things might have gone a little too far. If Anvi was so confident that she was going to star in our show that she had already convinced her tycoon dad to buy advertising . . . Um, well, that was going to be a problem, because Lakshmi and I were planning on winning the tryouts. We had practiced all weekend. We were ready.

Ms. Puri strode to the front of the classroom, her face folded into a frown.

"We have a change of program," she announced. Her voice was clipped. "Mr. Bhatnagar is requesting all girl students to please proceed to the stage immediately. We will resume with maths class as soon as this"—I could swear I heard her mutter the words *rehearsal nonsense*—"is over."

"Girls!" Mr. Bhatnagar was clapping loudly to get everyone's attention. "We have very less time, *betas*! Line up! Line up!"

All the girls lined up in one row at the front of the stage, while the boys sat down on the amphitheater's stone steps. I saw Dhruv Gupta nudge his neighbor, then point at me and snicker. I looked down and tucked my loose shirttail back into my skirt.

Ms. Puri was standing to the side, leaning against a pillar and watching everything, her arms folded across her chest. Her face was still creased in a deep frown, but when she caught me watching her, she gave a little wink through her blue plastic glasses.

That's when Mr. Bhatnagar walked up to Lakshmi, who was standing next to me at the very end of the row of girls. He leaned forward and said something to her in Hindi. I couldn't understand, but I felt Lakshmi tense up.

Mr. Bhatnagar was pointing at the steps. He must have been telling her to go sit.

Lakshmi didn't say anything. She didn't move. She just stared at the ground. Then she gave her head a little shake.

"Is there some problem, Mr. Bhatnagar?" Ms. Puri had come up and was standing next to him.

"Er, no," Mr. Bhatnagar said. "It's just this new girl, she is not wanting to listen."

"Her name is Lakshmi," Ms. Puri said. She stared hard at Mr. Bhatnagar, who seemed to be getting flustered. He took off his glasses and started cleaning the lenses with the hem of his white kurta.

"It is simply . . . we have no place in the finale for one new girl," Mr. Bhatnagar said. He was having trouble meeting Ms. Puri's gaze. "We are already practicing for so much of time."

This reasoning made no sense. Lakshmi wasn't that new anymore. She'd been at Premium Academy almost as long as I had. And she'd been practicing the dance with all the rest of us.

"But surely, there is no harm in letting her audition?" Ms. Puri said. She was raising her eyebrows at Mr. Bhatnagar, her head tilted to one side.

"Er, no," Mr. Bhatnagar said. "No, I suppose not."

"All right then!" said Ms. Puri brightly. "That's sorted." As she turned, she gave Lakshmi and me a tight smile.

So, here's the good part:

We aced the dance tryout. I mean, we nailed it. Five spins in sync, no stopping, no stepping out of position. Everybody was shocked. I could tell because when the music stopped and Lakshmi and I were frozen in our final pose, the amphitheater went totally silent. I mean, you could have heard a pin drop. I glanced out over the audience and drippy-nosed Dhruv was sitting there with his buddies, just staring at us, his mouth hanging open. That's how amazing we were.

Finally, one person started clapping. It was Ms. Puri. She was still leaning against the pillar, but she was clapping loudly. And then a couple of the nicer girls in the class—Soumya Singh and her smart-girl friends—started clapping too. And then even Dhruv gave a whistle and a couple of his buddies stomped their feet, and that's when I realized that we had pulled it off. I looked over at Lakshmi. She was grinning this enormous grin and then she leaned over to me and held her fist up and I gave it a bump.

Here is the kinda bad (but also exciting) part:

Anvi and Prisha did not do so well. In fact, they messed up pretty badly. Prisha stepped out during one of the spins and Anvi looked a little wobbly herself. When they finished, nobody clapped. A couple of girls started whispering. Prisha looked like she might cry.

At the end of the tryouts, everyone was sitting on the stone steps, waiting for Mr. Bhatnagar to announce the winners. Lakshmi and I sat together in the middle. Soumya and her friends were next to us, Dhruv behind us. Prisha sat alone, off to the side, on the front step. Anvi must have gone to the washroom or something.

Mr. Bhatnagar had taken off his glasses and was massaging his temples with his fingers again. Ms. Puri walked up to him. She whispered something in his ear. He nodded wearily.

"We have exciting news, boys and girls!" Ms. Puri exclaimed. She was beaming. "The winners of the dance tryouts are new members of our community! Let us all give a round of applause to Chloe and Lakshmi!"

Even though I knew we had nailed the routine and totally deserved to be selected, I was still stunned to hear our names said out loud. And then Lakshmi hugged me and Soumya and her friends were clapping us on the backs. Even Dhruv gave me a high five.

"All right, all right," said Ms. Puri. "It's over now. Back to maths, everyone." There was a communal groan. Then we all got up and started shuffling out of the amphitheater, toward the classroom.

Now here's the *really* bad part:

I was so stunned, I had to go to the washroom to splash some water on my face and make sure that everything was really happening. As I stood there, filling my cupped hands with water from the tap, someone came up next to me.

It was Anvi. She smiled at me in the mirror but it was one of those non-smiles—the corners of her mouth turned up but her eyes stayed the same.

"Congratulations, Chloe," Anvi said, but it didn't sound like she was congratulating me. It sounded like she was firing me as her friend.

"Um, thanks," I said. My hands were full now, so I had no choice but to splash the water over my face. When I straightened up, the water dripped, leaving wet splotches on the front of my uniform.

Her eyes had narrowed to little slits. She combed her fingers through her hair. "I have to say, I was surprised to see you up there with that girl," she said. "I didn't realize you two were such good friends."

"Um," I said. "Well . . ." I checked the towel dispenser: no paper towels. I wiped my face with my sleeve instead.

"Well, what?" Anvi said. Her eyes narrowed.

"Well, um, we're not really friends," I said.

"Oh," she said. "You looked like friends. You looked like *good* friends. And you must have practiced together." She paused. "When did you practice?"

At that moment, I didn't want Anvi to know that Lakshmi had been coming over to my house after school. I didn't want her to know that she had met my family and had snacks with me and played with my stuff. I didn't want her to know that we did origami together. I didn't want her to know that it was Lakshmi who had taught me the spins. That we had practiced in my room all weekend.

"No," I said, shaking my head. "We're definitely not friends."

"Okay," Anvi said. "Just checking." She lowered her voice. "You're not from here," she said, "so you may not know, but her father is a *mali.*" Anvi wrinkled her nose in disgust. "And who knows what her mother is. It's probably worse."

If I had been someone else—like my dad or Anna—I would have stopped her right there. I would have said "So what?" or "Who cares?" If I had been my mom, I would have hurled a question back in her face, something like "Could you explain to me the relevance of that statement?" or even,

"That seems to make you uncomfortable. Could you tell me why?"

But I am not my mom or my dad or my sister Anna. I'm just me.

And so I said, "Oh, okay."

Anvi gave me one last non-smile, then turned on her heel and walked out.

You can guess what happened next because it is the *absolutely* worst part:

Lakshmi opened a stall door. She just stood there, staring at me.

My mind was racing. Maybe she hadn't heard? We were talking in English pretty fast. Maybe she hadn't understood?

But then Lakshmi walked over to the sink next to mine and washed her hands slowly, pretending like I wasn't there. When she shook her hands dry, some drops of water flicked onto my sleeve.

And then she walked out.

Without saying a word.

That's how I knew she had heard and understood everything.

Chapter 20

After school, Lakshmi did not come to the park.

I waited for a long time, sitting on the grass, my back against our champa tree.

I had brought a ziplock bag of Lakshmi's favorite candies: gold coin chocolates and silver-wrapped toffees. There were even some gummies shaped like worms for Kali. After an hour of waiting, the chocolate had melted a bit and gotten stuck to the worm gummies. The candies were one messy clump.

I waited for another half hour. It was getting dark. I threw the bag of candy in the trash and headed home.

Chapter 21

I woke up the next morning with a bad feeling in the pit of my stomach.

I lay in bed for a long time, staring at the water stain on the ceiling and listening to the singsong of the wallahs as they bicycled past my window, advertising their wares: "Pomegranates! Papaya! Bananas! Pomegranates!"

My brain was spinning over everything that I had said in the bathroom, repeating it in an endless loop.

I had been so stupid, so cowardly, so wrong.

And now I was worried about the Annual Day performance. It was tomorrow night. How could I do it without Lakshmi? This was our special moment. The two of us together. We had practiced so hard. . . .

I was standing at the counter, spreading Nutella on my toast, when Mom burst into the kitchen. She raised her eyebrows in surprise to see me up and dressed so early.

"You okay?" she asked, giving me a quick peck on the cheek.

I just nodded.

Mom was wearing pearls and a business suit—always a bad sign.

She asked Anna, who was sitting at the kitchen table eating yogurt, to fasten her watch for her while she chugged some coffee. She was definitely in a rush.

That's when she let the bomb drop.

"Girls, I have a meeting with the minister of housing today. I need the car, so you'll have to take the school bus home. In fact, I think it would be a good idea for you to take it every day from now on. I need Vijay for work." She grabbed a dish towel off the counter and dabbed at the corners of her mouth, trying not to smudge her lipstick. "Besides, I think we're more of a bus family."

"What's that supposed to mean?" I dropped my knife in the sink. It clattered loudly. "I don't wanna take the bus."

Mom grabbed her keys off the counter. "I don't have time for this right now, Chloe. We can discuss it tonight when I get home."

"Where's Dad?" I said. I was not going to let this go without a fight.

"He's gone to Mumbai. He's back tomorrow night."

"But tomorrow's Annual Day!" I said.

"Oh, shit," Mom said.

"Mom!" Anna protested. She doesn't like swearing, especially from grown-ups.

"Sorry," Mom said. She glanced down at her BlackBerry. "Listen, Chloe, I'll talk to Dad. He'll catch an earlier flight home."

"You guys cannot miss this, Mom," I said. "It's really important."

Anna, for once, agreed with me. "It's pretty much the biggest school event of the year."

Mom kissed us both on the foreheads and then wiped at the lipstick smudges she must have left behind. "Don't worry, pumpkin," she said, leaning down to look into my eyes. "We'll all be there for your big event." She smiled. "Even Shreya's coming. We can't wait to see you dance with Lakshmi."

I looked down at my feet. I *had* told Mom and Dad about winning the dance tryout with Lakshmi. I *had not* told them about backstabbing her in the bathroom afterward. I just couldn't bring myself to do it. They were too proud of my "clever ploy" and "frankly heroic scheme" to help Lakshmi fit in with the class. Those were the actual words they used. The prouder they seemed, the worse I felt. How could I tell them what was really going on?

First thing at school that morning, we had two straight hours of dance practice. It was a fiasco, which is a fancy word for total-and-complete mess. Lakshmi wouldn't even look at me. We kept falling out of step. We were like two toy tops spinning at different angles.

Finally Mr. Bhatnagar took us aside. "What happened, *betas?*" he said. "Yesterday, you did the spins so nicely. Today, you cannot do them even once!"

Lakshmi and I stared at the ground.

Mr. Bhatnagar took off his glasses and ran his fingers over his bald head. He put his glasses back on. "The performance is tomorrow night." His voice had gone hard. "I don't know what is happening, but you two must figure it out or you will ruin the show." He glared down at us. "Is that what you want, *na?* To disappoint your teachers, your families, your friends?"

We shook our heads.

"*Chalo,* then. Take it from the top."

To make matters worse, over the course of the day, I grew more and more anxious about the bus. I'd never taken a school bus before—in Boston, we walked to school—and I didn't know what to expect. Who would be on the bus? How would I know where to get off? What if I missed my stop? For once, I was relieved that Anna would be there with me.

When the final bell rang and Anna and I climbed onto the bus, the only person already there was the bus monitor: a grumpy-looking assistant teacher with orange lipstick and earbuds plugged into her ears. She nodded at us and then went back to her iPhone. She was sitting in the front row, so we took the row directly behind her. Anna sat on one side of the aisle, I sat on the other.

I looked out the window to see who else would be coming. My heart soared when I saw Lakshmi walking toward us. She was surrounded by a group of other kids, all various ages and sizes, kids I had never noticed in school before. They all piled onto the bus, laughing and chattering away in Hindi. It surprised me. I had never seen Lakshmi with these kids. I had never seen her with anyone but Meher.

Lakshmi didn't see me until she was standing in the aisle right next to my seat and then she jolted like she had gotten an electric shock. I smiled at her, hopeful for a moment that she might sit down next to me, but she continued down the aisle without a word. At the very back of the bus, she settled in between two other girls with long, thick braids tied with navy-blue bows, exactly like hers. They looked like triplets, in their matching uniforms and matching braids and matching dark brown skin. Lakshmi whispered something to each of them and then they all stared at me till I turned around. I was facing forward, but I could feel their eyes on the back of my head. Had she told them about what happened in the bathroom yesterday? About what I had done?

As the rest of the kids boarded the bus, I stared out the window, chewing hard on my bottom lip so that I wouldn't cry. I could hear Lakshmi chattering away in the back. When I snuck a peek, she was breaking her *chikki,* left over from school lunch, into little pieces and handing them to her friends. A boy leaned over and said something to her and she let out one of her earth-shattering cackles.

Lakshmi had a whole group of friends, but I had nobody. Not Anvi. Not Lakshmi. Not even Katie back home. (Are you really friends if you can only Skype—and then lie the whole time that you do it?) Even Katie felt like a stranger to me now.

I had nobody. Nobody at all.

I bit my lip harder.

The bus coughed and lurched forward, out of the school gate.

If you're imagining a cheerful yellow school bus with big glass windows and wide padded seats, guess again. This bus was a tin can on wheels. The outside had once been white but was now so scraped and rusted and dented you could hardly tell. *Compresed Naturel Gaz* was painted in wobbly script across one side. The windows were iron bars. The only outward indication that it was a school bus was a small, hand-painted signboard propped up next to the Sai Baba figurine on the dashboard: the outline of a boy and girl wearing backpacks and holding hands. The girl had long braids like Lakshmi's.

The padding on the seats was so thin, I could feel the hard metal bars underneath. I found myself tensing over every bump and pothole, bracing myself for the bang to my spine. I've always suffered from car sickness and, as we swung around corners, the exhaust that filtered through the bus made my stomach sour.

Anna didn't seem to mind. She kept her nose in her Hindi recitation book, trying to memorize a poem for homework.

I don't think she looked up once. She hadn't even noticed Lakshmi.

After what felt like an eternity, we finally came to the first stop.

"Jhuggi!" yelled the driver. He wore a maroon-colored turban, and his scraggly beard was so long, it dangled through the gaps in the steering wheel.

His voice came out like a scratch. *"Chalo, chalo!"* he yelled.

All the kids from the back—Lakshmi and her gang of friends—trotted to the front of the bus and tumbled down the steps, still laughing and chatting with each other in Hindi. Lakshmi didn't even say bye to me. She never even looked my way.

As my eyes followed her through the barred window, I suddenly realized that we were at the same traffic light where Vijay always got stuck. I craned my neck to see out Anna's side. Yep, we were across the street from the slum.

Then it dawned on me: this is where Lakshmi lives.

Chapter 22

"Chloe?"

Anna and I were walking home from the bus stop. It was Wednesday afternoon—T minus three hours till curtain—and my life was officially a disaster. Remember *fiasco*? That's an even better word. My life was a fiasco. Everything had fallen apart.

Ever since the bathroom incident on Monday, Lakshmi had been ignoring me. I had lost her as a friend. Anvi was ignoring me, too. She couldn't believe that I had "stolen" her spot in the Annual Day finale. As for that finale, it was now in jeopardy. Lakshmi was threatening to quit.

It was Meher who told me. She had snuck up on me as I was about to board the bus after school. She tugged on my shirtsleeve, pulling me toward a clump of bushes behind the bus.

"What *is* it, Meher?" I said, shaking her off. "What do you want?"

The exhaust pipe was belching black smoke. I coughed. "I need to get on the bus."

"It Lakshmi," Meher said. "She quit."

"What?"

"She quit Annual Day dance. She not do show."

"But we practiced all day," I said. "We were actually okay."

It was true—today's practice had been miles better than yesterday's. Lakshmi still wouldn't look at me. She never smiled, never made eye contact, but at least we managed to perform the spins at pretty much the same time. Even Mr. Bhatnagar had clapped us on the backs, saying we were ready for the performance.

Meher was shaking her head. She looked like she might cry. "No, no, she tell me she bunking tonight." Meher tugged on my sleeve again. "You talk to Lakshmi, Chloe! You tell her she come. She must do the show!"

But Lakshmi hadn't shown up for the bus ride home. That's when I suspected that Meher was telling the truth.

The whole bus ride, I stared out the window, going over the facts in my head. My conclusion: this was all my fault. I was the one who had backstabbed Lakshmi in the bathroom. Now she was abandoning us at the last possible moment, just a few hours before the performance. This was her payback. She knew how nervous I was. She knew I needed her there. She knew I couldn't do the spins alone. And she didn't care enough about everybody else—about Anvi and Meher and Dhruv and the rest of the class. All she really cared about was me, and I had failed her. I had failed Mom and Dad. I had failed everybody.

"Chloe?"

We were on our way home from the bus stop. I had been trudging along behind Anna, but now she stopped on the side of the street by the park across from our house. Her arms were crossed over her chest. She glared at me.

"You've been sulking for days," she said. "You might as well spit it out. I'm just going to wait here till you do."

My chin started to tremble.

"Uh-oh," she said, her voice more gentle. "Here, let's find a bench."

She tucked one hand under my elbow and pulled me through the park gate and over to a bench. It happened to be facing the champa trees, which only made me cry harder. The last two days, I had rushed home to change, then gone right back out to this very spot in the park, hoping that Lakshmi would show up. I had waited here for hours on Monday and Tuesday. But Lakshmi never came.

Anna sat quietly next to me while I blubbered. She didn't try to hug me or talk to me, she just unzipped the side pocket of her backpack and handed me a small packet of Kleenex. She offered me a sip from her stainless steel water bottle, too.

"Now tell me what's going on," Anna said.

So that's when I admitted to everything that had happened:

the tryouts on Monday, the bathroom scene afterward, be-traying Lakshmi. "And now Meher says she won't do the per-formance tonight," I said. "She's not going to show up. And I can't do it without her, Anna! I can't make it through. The whole show will be ruined. And it's all my fault!"

Anna looked at me gravely. "There is a way to fix this," she said. "And it's actually pretty simple."

"Huh?" I blew my nose. "What do you mean? What is it?"

"I think you know," Anna said.

"Well, what would *you* do?"

Anna cocked her head. "You and I are different people, right?" she said.

Even when we were babies, Anna and I were opposites. Mom says I came out all chubby and giggly whereas Anna was skinny and colicky. I loved music; Anna liked quiet. I liked to be outside; Anna wanted to stay in her playpen.

As we grew older, the gap only widened. Back in Boston, we shared a room, which nearly drove Anna crazy because I would leave my bed unmade and dump my dirty clothes on the floor. Anna fluffed her pillows every morning and hung her clothes up in the closet at night. Sometimes I'd install myself on our toilet, door open, reading comic books, my sweatpants pooled around my ankles. Anna peed with the door closed.

Anna was the family's good girl; I was the troublemaker. Once, when I stole a packet of M&M's from the corner deli, it was Anna who made me go back and apologize.

Plus, we've always looked like opposites. Anna has Dad's dark brown hair and serious eyes. I'm blond like Mom. She has long, graceful limbs; I'm stocky. Mom calls us Snow White and Rose Red, like the sisters in the Grimms' fairy tale. That's how different we are.

"So what *I* would do doesn't really matter, does it?" Anna was saying. "You have to do what's right for *you.*"

"But sometimes it's hard to know—you know?" I said. I had stopped crying. Now I was plucking the petals off a champa flower and dropping them one by one onto the grass.

"I know." Anna nodded.

I glanced over at her. "You do?" I said. "Because it seems like you never do anything wrong."

Anna let out a little laugh. "That's not true," she said. She paused for a beat. "You remember when Mom freaked out because she couldn't find our plane tickets and we were gonna miss our flight to Delhi?"

I nodded.

"That was me," she said.

"What?"

"I ripped them up and hid them in the recycling."

"No way!" I said. I couldn't believe it.

"Yep," Anna said. She had her lips pressed together in a smile, deep dimples grooved into her cheeks. Then she looked out over the park and sighed. "Too bad it didn't work," she added.

"You mean . . . You don't like it here?" I said. "You have so many friends. I thought you loved it!"

Anna gave me a funny look. "I'm just making the best of it, Chloe," she said. "Sometimes that's what you have to do."

"But . . ." I was having trouble digesting all this new

information. "But you're a uniform monitor. And you always get good grades. And you go to the mall with your new friends. You even speak Hindi!"

"I don't really like the mall," Anna said.

"Oh."

"And my Hindi stinks. But this isn't about me, Chloe," she continued. "It's about you and Lakshmi. What are you going to do?"

"Um, run away?"

Anna let out another laugh. "I don't think that's a viable option," she said. "Besides, what about Annual Day? Don't you want to be in the show? This is your big moment— yours and Lakshmi's."

I nodded. In my heart of hearts, I *did* want to be in the Annual Day performance. I wanted to wear the sparkly costume and put on makeup and stand backstage, listening to the murmur of the audience until the lights dimmed and the music came on and I stepped out. . . .

"Well, then I think you better apologize," Anna was saying. "Which means we need to find Lakshmi." She looked at her wristwatch. "And we have only about forty-five minutes till you have to start getting ready for the show."

"We?" I said. "You mean, you're gonna help?"

Anna nodded.

I looked at my sister, sitting there in her neat school uniform, her dark brown hair tucked up in its high ponytail. Suddenly, my heart was filled with hope.

I leapt up from the bench. "Well," I said, "I think I might know where we can find her."

Chapter 23

I had no idea how sneaky my big sister could be till I heard her tell Dechen that she needed to take me to the market, quick, to buy some bindis for my Annual Day costume.

Dechen glanced up from the chopping board, her eyes narrow.

"Now you helping your sister?" she said. She sounded suspicious.

Anna put one arm around my shoulders. "Sure," she said. "Why not?"

Dechen just shook her head and went back to chopping.

Vijay took a little more convincing. He had dropped Mom at her interview and was killing time, drinking chai on the street with the neighbor's security guards, till he had to go back to pick her up. He glanced down at his watch, frowning. "Then we go *jaldi jaldi, betas,*" he said, gulping down the last of his tea.

Now we were double-parked beside the market, a small

pedestrian area with a dry goods store, a butcher, a couple of pharmacies, a fruit and vegetable wallah, and one long row of tailors, all stooped over their whirring sewing machines. Vijay was hesitating. He didn't want us to go into the market alone, but there were no parking spots and the traffic was backing up behind us.

"I take you inside," he said.

Some cars honked angrily.

"Don't worry, Vijay, we'll be quick," Anna said. "And you need to stay with the car." She opened the door and started to get out before Vijay could protest further. "We'll be ten minutes," she said. "We'll meet you right back here."

I jumped out behind her and she slammed the door shut.

"Quick!" Anna grabbed my arm and pulled me past the row of tailors, their heads bent under the hot afternoon sun, and around the corner by the fruit wallah, where a dirt path I had never noticed before stretched behind the market to the slum beyond.

"How do you know about this?" I asked.

Anna shrugged. "I keep my eyes open. Now come on. We don't have much time."

She started walking down the path.

"I dunno, Anna," I said. There was garbage strewn along both sides of the path—old plastic bags and bottles and *paan* wrappers everywhere. The skeleton of a bicycle lay off to one side, its pedal-less crank arm sticking out like an amputated limb. Farther down the path, two enormous pigs were shuffling around a mound of garbage, their snouts sniffing hungrily. They looked bigger than Igor and Bruno, the twin mastiffs that lived next door to us in Boston. Long, stringy hairs grew from the pigs' blotchy skin.

Anna stopped in the middle of the path and glared at me. "This is where Lakshmi *lives*, Chloe," she said. "I think you can handle ten minutes of it. Now come on!" She turned and started back down the path.

Who knew she could be so tough?

I took a deep breath and held it, trying to block out the stench of garbage and worse: the small clearing we passed that reeked of poop. I buried my nose in my elbow, trying not to gag. It must have been the slum's open-air bathroom.

Anna picked up the pace, jogging past the clearing, till we came to the edge of the *basti,* where she stopped and took a deep breath.

"That was gross!" I said.

"Shhh!" she admonished.

A couple of little kids were standing there, staring at us. They wore no shoes. Their clothes and faces and limbs were smudged with dirt. One girl's skirt was so ripped, I could see her underwear. Her hair was matted in clumps against her head. Snot ran from her nostrils to her upper lip like the thick slime trail left by a slug.

"Lakshmi?" Anna said. She squatted down so that she was eye level with the little girl. *"Aap Lakshmi ko janate ho?"*

The girl just stared at Anna with big, unblinking brown eyes.

Just then, a group of older boys came around the corner.

They wore *chappals* and T-shirts with logos tucked into their shorts. They looked less dirty than the first group of kids. One carried a cricket bat over his shoulder. They stopped short when they saw us.

"Hello, madam!" the boy with the cricket bat exclaimed. He gave Anna a broad grin. His two front teeth were missing.

"He speaks English!" I said to Anna.

"Wouldn't count on it," Anna muttered.

The boys gathered around us, nudging each other and whispering in Hindi.

"Do you know Lakshmi?" Anna spoke slowly, enunciating every word.

"Lakshmi?" the boy with the cricket bat echoed. For some reason, the other boys found this hysterical. They started cracking up. "Lakshmi?" they repeated over and over. "Lakshmi?"

"They're making fun of you!" I whispered.

"Yeah, I get that, Chloe," Anna said. "Here"—she grabbed my elbow and started walking—"let's keep going."

As we stepped into the *basti,* the two groups of kids followed on our heels, like we were pied pipers. They chattered excitedly to each other in Hindi. Every once in a while, one of the older boys would yell "Hello!" or "You English?"

I wished they wouldn't cram in so close to us.

Both sides of the dirt path were now lined with small slum houses made of brick. Some were partially plastered and some were painted bright colors—turquoise and aqua green—though the paint was chipped and peeling. Most had sheet metal roofs, but some were covered with only sticks and tarps and flattened cardboard boxes. Those ones didn't have satellite dishes. Electrical wires hung like spiderwebs over our heads.

Most of the front doors were propped open, probably because of the heat. As we walked, I tried to peek inside, but the sun was so bright and the houses so dark, I couldn't see much. As far as I could tell, they were all just one room with little or no furniture, though I saw a couple of TVs parked on packed-earth floors. In one house an old woman was squatting over a small gas cooking range, stirring something in a metal pot. When she caught me watching her, she tugged at her sari to cover her face.

We had reached the end of the path. Now it split into several branches, each one winding deeper into the slum. Anna stopped at the intersection and peered down each lane, hesitating. The kids stopped too, waiting to see what we'd do next. Then the boy with the cricket bat reached his hand out and touched my hair.

I jumped. "He's touching me!"

"Just stay calm, Chloe," Anna said, but her voice sounded tight.

"But where are we going?" I said. "Which way do we go? How do we find Lakshmi? What if we get lost?"

"Give me a minute to think. . . ."

"I help you?" An old man in white kurta-pajamas was sitting cross-legged on a charpoy in front of a brick hut. He had a thick black mustache. It twitched when he spoke.

"Yes, please!" Anna said. "These kids . . ." She waved her hand at the children who had been following us.

The man barked something in Hindi and the kids took a few steps back.

"You not from here," the man observed. He was holding a small plastic cup of chai and when he sipped from it, his hand quivered.

"No," Anna said. "Actually, we're looking for a girl, a friend." She held her hand at chest level to indicate Lakshmi's height. "Her name is Lakshmi?"

The old man pointed at Anna's chest with one shaky finger.

"Premium Academy?" he said.

Anna glanced down at the crest embroidered on the front pocket of her uniform. "Yes!" she said. "She goes to Premium Academy. She is the *mali's* daughter. Lakshmi. Do you know her? Do you know Lakshmi?"

The old man smiled. His teeth were surprisingly white, like his kurta. "Very good school." He nodded approvingly. "Very good school." He took another wobbly sip of chai.

"But Lakshmi?" Anna prodded.

"Yes, Lakshmi," the old man echoed. He dropped the plastic cup on the ground and then unfolded himself slowly from his charpoy. "We go."

He started down the left-hand alleyway. We hesitated for a moment—the group of kids had crowded back close to us—but the old man turned and shooed them away and then beckoned for us to follow him.

As we walked deeper into the *basti,* the paths grew narrower and more winding, with smaller huts packed closer together. There was sewage flowing through uncovered channels.

I felt eyes on me. Men seemed to be everywhere—leaning in doorways or sitting on cane chairs, talking on cell phones, drinking tea, or chewing *paan* and spitting as we passed. They watched us, but didn't say anything.

I held Anna's hand.

Only the women were working—squatting in the dirt to roll out chapatis on wooden boards or to squeeze laundry in plastic tubs. Some young girls passed us, balancing water jugs on their heads. They reminded me of that pretty girl I had seen in the pink *lehenga,* struggling to cross the street with her heavy water jugs. So much had happened in just a few months. I never imagined I would be walking right here in this very same . . .

The old man had come to an abrupt stop. He peered around the corner, then ducked back and waved us over to the side. He pressed his body against the wall of a hut, so we did the same, hiding in the shadow of its corrugated metal roof.

"Shhh!" he said.

"What's going on?" I said to Anna. "What's happening?"

"I don't know," she whispered.

"Shhh!" the old man insisted. "Some goondas are there!"

Our bodies pressed against the hut, we could now hear deep voices barking in rapid-fire Hindi.

"I don't know about this, Anna," I whispered. "Maybe we should get out of here."

The old man was peeking around the corner again, but he kept one hand back, gesturing for us to stay put.

"Just wait a—" But before Anna could finish her sentence, the old man had spun on his heel and shoved her hard on the shoulder. Anna slammed against me. He pushed her again and we both stumbled through the open door of the little hut. Anna tripped over me and we fell to the ground. We lay there, sprawled on the dirt floor, too stunned to speak. When I looked up, the old man was blocking the open door with his thin body. He was facing us, his back to the outside. I was about to say something—to protest—but he glared down at me and then placed one crooked index finger against his lips, signaling for me to keep quiet.

Anna and I stayed there, frozen in a heap on the floor, not speaking. As my eyes slowly adjusted to the darkness inside the hut—there were no windows, the only light coming from the doorway—I saw a little girl crouched in the corner. She had to be three, maybe four. Someone had outlined her eyes in thick black *kajal*. She stared at me with huge, unblinking raccoon eyes.

What if she yelled? What if she called out?

I forced a smile.

Then I heard footsteps outside.

I peeked between the old man's ankles just in time to catch a glimpse of two muscular men in dark gray uniforms and mirrored sunglasses as they strode by.

I shook my head, confused.

The Saxenas' security guards? What were *they* doing here?

As soon as the men had rounded the corner, the old man reached down to help me and Anna up from the floor. We dusted ourselves off, stepping back out into the lane.

"So sorry, I see goondas, I . . ."

But we didn't wait to hear his explanation. I spotted a familiar figure coming around the corner.

"Lakshmi!" I ran forward and threw my arms around her skinny waist.

Kali appeared out of nowhere and stuck her nose between us. She barked and pawed at Lakshmi, trying to free her from my embrace.

"Chloe?" Lakshmi said, shaking me loose. "What you doing here?" She leaned down and stroked Kali, trying to calm her. The dog sat down on her foot.

"Anna?" Lakshmi was looking back and forth, from me to my sister.

"Lakshmi, what's going on?" Anna said. "Is everything okay?"

A group of men were clustered nearby, arguing in Hindi. Their voices were angry and they were gesticulating wildly. One was gripping his hair with both hands. He looked like he was going to cry.

A group of women behind them *was* crying, letting out loud wails that set off tears in the babies they clutched to their hips. It was pandemonium.

"Here, come," Lakshmi said. She pulled me by the hand toward a small house. It was brick like the others but painted a bright spring green. Anna and I stepped inside. The interior walls were whitewashed, but the floor was gray concrete. The only pieces of furniture were a metal trunk and a small bookshelf crammed with dictionaries and workbooks I recognized from school. The top of the bookshelf was covered in old Thums Up bottles filled with plant cuttings. In one corner was the kitchen: a gas cylinder, a two-burner cooking range, and a red plastic bucket full of water. A metal frying pan and some cooking utensils hung from nails hammered into the wall. There was only one picture in the whole place—a photo of a young couple, sitting stiffly in their wedding clothes. The woman wasn't smiling, but she had Lakshmi's laughing eyes.

"Please," Lakshmi was saying. She pointed at our feet. "Your shoes."

"Oh, sorry." We slipped off our school shoes and placed them in the doorway.

Kali was sitting sentinel outside, her back straight and ears up. She reminded me of the foo dogs outside our favorite Chinese take-out place in Boston. I stifled a giggle. It was my nerves. This whole crazy afternoon was getting to me.

Lakshmi had pulled a collapsed cardboard box into the middle of the room. She motioned for Anna and me to sit on it, so we did.

My eyes landed on the logo printed on one corner of the

box: a smiley face with LIFE'S GOOD in cheerful pink letters underneath.

Really? I thought. *Life is good? Here?*

"You take water?" Lakshmi gestured to the red bucket.

Anna shook her head. "No, thanks. We're fine."

Lakshmi sat down cross-legged on the floor in front of us.

"What's going on, Lakshmi?" Anna said. "Who were those men? And why are all those women crying?"

Lakshmi bit her lip.

"C'mon, Lakshmi." Anna put her hand on Lakshmi's knee. "You can tell us."

Lakshmi picked at the end of one of her braids for a moment. Finally, she spoke. "These goondas, they come. You see them?"

We nodded.

"One smaller and one big, big man. He even have gun." Lakshmi puffed out her chest and pointed her index finger toward her hip, as though putting a revolver in a holster. "My father, he not here. He outside. Working at school— you know?—making preparation for Annual Day . . ."

We nodded.

"This big goonda, he say my father house—this house—um . . ." Lakshmi hesitated, searching for the right word. "He say our house not with law."

"Not legal?" Anna said. "It's illegal?"

"Yes!" Lakshmi said. "He say our house illegal. This DDA land—Delhi Development Authority."

"Okay . . . ," Anna said.

"He say I do dancing and they take this land—our house and our neighbor houses—and they build megamall this place."

"What?"

Lakshmi swung one arm in a digging motion. "Machine," she said. "One big machine is coming next day. One—"

"Wait, hold on, back up," Anna said. "What's this about dancing? What exactly did the man say?"

"He say I quit Annual Day." Lakshmi shrugged. "I not do dancing."

"But *why?*" Anna was shaking her head, trying to understand. "Let me get this straight: if you participate in the Annual Day show, someone is going to come tomorrow and demolish your home?"

Lakshmi nodded.

"This guy was threatening you?" Anna persisted.

I couldn't help myself. "Meher told me, Lakshmi," I burst out. "She said you already quit the show, that you weren't going to show up tonight anyway. Is that right? Were you really going to skip out on us?"

"Are you kidding me, Chloe?" Anna glared at me. "Lakshmi just told us her home is about to be bulldozed and all you can think about is your stupid dance routine?"

"It is okay," Lakshmi said to Anna. She placed one hand on my forearm. It felt cool and rough. "Chloe," she said quietly.

I nodded.

"It not matter what happen between us. I cannot go to

show tonight. I cannot do dance. Before, I did not want to and now I really cannot. I already tell goondas I stay here. I cannot let them touch my father house. Not after everything. Not after . . ." Lakshmi paused for a moment. Tears filled her eyes. She lowered her head. In all my time with Lakshmi, I had never seen her cry.

"Lakshmi?"

She raised her eyes to mine.

I hesitated for a moment.

"One of those guys—the big one—did he have a tattoo on his arm?"

Lakshmi nodded slowly.

Anna stared at me.

"A tattoo of a dagger?"

Lakshmi nodded again, faster.

"With a curved, pointy end?"

"Yes!"

"Chloe!" Anna jumped in. "What on earth? What's going on? Do you know those guys?"

"I think I know who they are," I said. "And I think I know who's behind them, who's threatening Lakshmi's house. And I think I know why. Which means I might know how to stop them too."

It was like what happens in cartoons: a lightbulb had come on in my head.

I turned to Lakshmi. "But you'll have to trust me, Lakshmi. Can you trust me?"

Lakshmi and Anna were both staring at me like I was

crazy. But I wasn't. In fact, a plan was already piecing itself together in my mind.

"Can you trust me, Lakshmi?" I repeated.

There was a long pause.

"First you tell me," she finally said. "Then I decide if I trust you, Chloe."

I nodded. "Okay," I said. "That's fair."

And then I told them everything I knew.

Chapter 24

Anna was doing my makeup in the bathroom when we heard pebbles on the window: *tap, tap, tap.* She checked her wristwatch: six o'clock on the dot, just as we planned.

I ran to the window and waved to Lakshmi. She pointed to her dad's bike and then to the side of the house—she would hide the bike around the corner. I gave her a thumbs-up.

Mom was at her computer and Dad was helping Dechen wrestle Lucy into her pajamas, so Anna and I snuck downstairs without anyone noticing. While Anna distracted Vijay, I eased the car trunk open and beckoned to Lakshmi. She dashed over and slipped into the trunk, folding herself up like an umbrella to fit behind the backseat. She had to put her head on Vijay's motorcycle helmet and wedge his tiffin under her knees. Good thing she was so skinny.

I eased the trunk closed, wincing as it clicked, but Vijay

didn't seem to notice. As I headed back up the stairs, I gave Anna a thumbs-up behind Vijay's back.

Phase one complete.

Mom and Dad were treating Annual Day like a big family occasion. Mom made me pose for a bunch of photos in my costume and full makeup. I had so much eyeliner and sparkly eye shadow on that it looked like I was dressed for Halloween. She herself was wearing a brand-new kurta and dangly earrings. Dad wore a tie. He had made himself and Mom a gin and tonic each before we set out, so they were in high spirits, chatting away in the car.

"Here's the irony," Mom was saying. "He's the minister of housing and urban poverty alleviation and we pull up and he's got this Lutyens bungalow on—what do you think, Vijay?—maybe two acres? I mean, he's drowning in green lawns. Flowers are everywhere. It was just like Shreya said it would be. He even served me tea on the veranda!"

"So, you got a good quote for the story?"

Mom grinned and rubbed her hands together. She reminded me of Lucy when you put a bowl of ice cream in front of her. She was practically drooling. "Oh, it gets even better. He gives me this whole speech about how he's going to make Delhi slum-free in five years. I mean, he's handing the story to me on a silver platter. . . ."

I exchanged a smile with Anna. This was too good.

We parked and I distracted Mom and Dad by asking them to take a photo of me with Vijay, while Anna snuck around to the back of the car and let Lakshmi out of the trunk. As we walked toward the school's front gates, I kept glancing back to make sure Lakshmi was following us. There she was, keeping to the shadows.

"You nervous, honey?" Dad said. He took my hand.

"Uh, why?"

"'Cause you keep glancing around . . ." Dad gave me a funny look.

"Just looking for friends," I said. (It wasn't a complete lie.)

Mom put her arm around my shoulders. "We're so proud of you, Chloe," she said. "You're adjusting so well to school, making all these new friends."

"Thanks, Mom," I said.

Families were streaming toward the school gates, moms decked out in sparkly saris, dads in designer jeans.

There was excitement in the air. The school was floodlit and festooned with garlands of yellow and orange marigolds. Huge sponsorship banners covered the facade. I glanced up and spotted Anvi's, looming above the others:

Congratulations to Anvi
Our Little Shining Star!
From Papa, Mama & Saxena Enterprises LLC
Growing India One Mega-Luxury Experience At A Time

Mrs. Anand was positioned at the entrance in a red sari with gold trim, welcoming parents.

She smiled when she saw us. "I understand Chloe is making a special contribution tonight," she said.

A gong sounded.

"Please take your seats," Mrs. Anand said, ushering us toward the amphitheater. "Chloe, you may join your class backstage. Anna, I have one special job for you. Please find me once you've deposited your sister."

Mom and Dad each gave me a kiss and then headed toward the theater to find Shreya. As soon as they melted into the crowd, Anna and I sprinted up to the second floor. It was empty except for Lakshmi, who was waiting for us in the supply closet. The plan was going smoothly.

"We did it!" I squealed as we hugged each other. "Oh, Lakshmi, you made it!"

"C'mon, Chloe," Anna said. "We'd better get you backstage. Lakshmi, I'll come back to do your costume and makeup as soon as I can."

Lakshmi nodded. Then she reached into her pockets and pulled out two long garlands of jasmine flowers. She handed one to me. "We wear these tonight," she said. "For my mama."

I nodded. The gong sounded again and Anna pulled me out of the closet.

Mr. Bhatnagar was pacing backstage.

"These people, they show no respect, no respect!" he muttered as he pushed and pulled us into position. "How could she do this? How *could* she not show up? I knew I shouldn't have picked her! You give them one chance and this is how they repay you! They should never be allowed in this school. Never!" He glared at Meher, who was sniffling in the corner.

Poor Meher. Lakshmi had wanted to let her in on our plan, but I said we couldn't risk it.

Mr. Bhatnagar walked over to Anvi and Prisha. His voice softened, "Here, *betas.* You come here." He pulled them forward, placing them first in line. "Now *you* will have to be our stars tonight. You will save the show for us, won't you? You will do the spins?"

Anvi and Prisha nodded, flashing him angelic smiles.

As soon as he turned away, Anvi put her lips by my ear. "You can't say I didn't warn you about them," she hissed, tilting her chin in Meher's direction.

I couldn't help but notice—Anvi looked gorgeous. Her black hair was in a special updo. Her makeup was perfect. And her mother must have hired a tailor to alter her costume, because it hugged her body, making her long, slender arms and legs even more spidery than usual.

I tugged at the fabric around my bum where the bulky costume bagged and sagged. I was like an elephant next to Anvi.

Anvi reached up and fingered the end of the jasmine garland, which Ms. Puri had strung through my pudgy blond ponytail. She raised her eyebrows. "This is pretty," she said. "Where'd you get it?"

Class Four was already halfway through its routine. My class was poised in the wings, ready to go on next. I was starting to sweat.

Where was Lakshmi?

Anna was supposed to get her and bring her backstage.

I craned my neck, trying to see up the back stairwell. They should have shown up by now. We had to cut it close, of course, but this was *too* close.

Where were they?

I looked around for Anna, but I couldn't see her, either. She was supposed to be an usher tonight. What if she got stuck somewhere?

"Looking for your sister?" Anvi whispered.

I nodded.

"She's with my parents."

"Huh?"

Anvi rolled her eyes. "The *guests of honor?*" she said. She pointed toward the balcony. "Up in the platinum sponsor box . . ."

I followed Anvi's finger. There was Anna, sitting on a raised platform way up in the balcony. She was perched on an armchair between Mrs. Anand and an oversized man in a sky-blue turban: Deepak Saxena. Anna's face was white. Her hands gripped the armrests.

I waved wildly.

"I don't think she can see you," Anvi said.

What could I do? How would I get Lakshmi? It was too late to leave. I'd miss my entrance.

I had no choice. I had to get help.

It took Ms. Puri about five seconds to understand what had happened. She sent the fastest boy in the class: Dhruv Gupta. He returned with Lakshmi just as our music was starting.

"Lakshmi!" I yelped.

I only wish I had had a camera to capture the look on Anvi's face when she turned and saw Lakshmi in full costume and makeup, sprinting down the stairs toward us. But there wouldn't have been time anyway. The music soared, the lights lowered, Lakshmi grabbed my hand, and we stepped out onto the stage together, hand in hand.

You know on TV, when they do a slow-motion replay and you see the football leaving the quarterback's fingers—spinning slowly, slowly in perfect spirals through the air? That's what it was like for me. Time stopped. There was just Lakshmi and me. The stage lights blazing down upon us. The music soaring. I saw her white teeth. Her black eyes, shining at me. I saw her skirt flare out as she spun on the stage. Her braids flying out around her. Lights, lights, lights.

The faces of the audience blurred together like cars whizzing by on the highway at night.

And then, bang. It was over.

We were frozen in our final pose. The music had stopped. The audience was cheering.

Lakshmi was saying something to me, reaching out for my hand so that we could step to the front of the stage and bow together.

She dropped my hand to curtsy by herself and the audience roared its appreciation.

It was obvious to everyone: she was the star that night.

"The spins, the spins! You did them, girls! They were perfect!"

Dad had managed to push his way through the crowd.

He and Mom gave us both huge hugs.

I introduced Lakshmi to Shreya, who wrapped her arms around both our waists, giving us tight squeezes.

"I've heard so much about you!" she said to Lakshmi, who was still grinning like crazy.

"You were wonderful, girls," Mom said. "Just wonderful."

"Is your dad here, Lakshmi?" Dad asked. "We'd love to meet him."

"Um . . ." Lakshmi and I exchanged glances, but before either of us could answer, Ms. Puri walked up. She had Dhruv beside her.

"Mr. and Mrs. Jones," she said, "thank you for bringing Lakshmi. I didn't know what to think when she didn't show up at first but then—"

"But we didn't," Mom interrupted. "We didn't bring Lakshmi."

"Here we go . . . ," I whispered.

All eyes turned to Lakshmi and me.

"We . . . um . . . I . . . ," I started to say.

"Chloe?" Mom said. Her voice was sharp. "Could you please tell us what is going on?"

"I can explain." Anna stepped forward.

Mom stared, one hand clamped over her mouth, trying not to interrupt as Anna told the whole story: how Lakshmi had planned on quitting the show, how we had gone to the *basti* to try to change her mind, how the goondas had shown up and threatened to tear down her home, Lakshmi's change of heart when I explained who they were. How we told her she couldn't let the Saxenas bully her into abandoning the show just so Anvi could steal the spotlight. She couldn't let them win.

Anna told them about how we had smuggled Lakshmi to school in the trunk of the car so that the goondas wouldn't know ("She was in the back, right behind us, during the whole ride?" Dad said. We all nodded.), how we had tricked everyone into thinking that Anvi and Prisha would star— until Lakshmi stepped onto the stage at the last possible moment. . . .

"When Anna not come, I sneak into washroom and do my hair and makeup and costume all by myself," Lakshmi said proudly. "And then I wait and I wait and I wait and then Dhruv Gupta come to get me. . . ."

"I couldn't believe it when Mrs. Anand told me to accompany the Saxenas to their seats," Anna said. "I was trapped up there! Thank God for Dhruv."

All eyes turned to Dhruv. He smiled sheepishly.

I couldn't tell if Mom was furious, so I just stood there, not saying anything, while Anna finished our story. "And so, I guess we all figured, given the article Chloe saw on your computer that night and your meeting with the housing minister yesterday, um, well . . . that you could . . . maybe, um . . . help us save the *basti*?"

There was a long silence as the four grown-ups digested this information. I held my breath. Now that I had heard Anna say it all out loud, this plan of mine sounded pretty far-fetched.

It was Shreya who finally broke the silence. "Lakshmi," she said, "can you take us to your house?"

Lakshmi nodded.

Shreya turned to Mom. She pointed at her camera. "Well, you've got your Nikon, Helen. Press credentials?"

Mom shook her head briefly, as though trying to wake herself from a dream.

"Um, they're in the car, but . . ."

"But what?" Shreya said. "We don't have much time."

That's when Dhruv Gupta laughed. "Now I see why you are so *mirchi, Chhole*. It's the company you keep!"

I punched him lightly on the arm. "You know I hate that nickname."

Dhruv grinned.

"But thanks," I added. "Thanks for helping get Lakshmi. And, um, congratulations on your Achievement Award. You deserve it."

Dhruv shrugged and then pointed to his parents, who were searching for him in the crowd. "Gotta go," he said. "Good luck, Lakshmi. Good luck, Chloe!" (Yes, he actually used my real name.) He disappeared into the crowd.

"All right, everyone! Let's go!" Shreya said. "I'll take my scooter and meet you there."

I looked over at Anna. She was clasping and unclasping her hands, like she does when she's working on a really tough math problem. "There's one more thing," she said, her voice tense. We all leaned forward.

"When Lakshmi came onstage, Anvi's dad made a phone call."

Lakshmi gripped my hand.

"I'm so sorry, Lakshmi." Anna shook her head. "I couldn't understand what he said—it was all in Hindi—but I could hear his voice. And he sounded angry."

Chapter 25

By the time we got to the *basti* it was after ten o'clock and pitch black. There was a silver Range Rover parked by the side of the road. As we pulled up behind it, Shreya screeched up next to us on her scooter.

"Hey, take a look at this!" Shreya grabbed Mom's Nikon and crouched down by the Range Rover's driver's-side door, trying to get a close-up shot of the crest emblazoned across it:

SAXENA ENTERPRISES LLC
THE MEGA-LUXURY EXPERIENCE

"They're here," Shreya said. "We better hurry."

She gave the camera back to Mom, then grabbed Lakshmi by the hand. The two of them started sprinting down the alley.

"I still can't believe this," Dad muttered as we took off behind them.

When we got to Lakshmi's house, there was no sign of the Saxenas' thugs. But there were two fat policemen surrounded by a crowd of *basti* dwellers. The cops were holding thick stacks of Delhi Development Authority signs. They had just slapped one sideways onto the front of Lakshmi's house. Lakshmi's dad was slumped in the doorway, watching them.

I will never in my life forget the look on those fat policemen's faces when they turned and saw Shreya and Lakshmi barreling toward them, hand in hand, the rest of us close behind. When Mom held up her Nikon, they shrank back, hands shielding their faces, like they were being blinded by a superhero.

Lakshmi flung herself into her father's arms. He hugged her and then looked up at the rest of us in confusion.

In his defense, we must have been a strange sight: Lakshmi and me in our sparkly dance outfits and full stage makeup, Anna in her uniform, Dad in his professor's glasses and tie, Mom with her camera. Shreya was shouting at the policemen in rapid-fire Hindi, shaking her finger in their startled faces. Even Vijay had come. He held a baseball bat by his side.

Brandishing a notebook, Shreya had switched to English and was now demanding the names of the two potbellied policemen, who were stammering like schoolchildren brought before the principal.

"The driver and passenger of the silver Range Rover SUV, license plate DL 2SAX 4189, parked on the main road?" Shreya barked. "I don't suppose you remember their names either?"

The crowd of *basti* dwellers must have suspected a turn in the tide of their fortunes because they started to jeer. Then someone threw a rock at the policemen.

"Girls"—Dad's voice was quiet but urgent—"let's go back to the car." He grabbed Anna and me by the elbows and tried to pull us back down the alley.

"But Mom and Shreya and Lakshmi . . . ," I protested, wriggling loose. I didn't want to leave them there by themselves.

"Vijay . . . ," Dad said.

Vijay nodded.

"Girls, you're coming with me. Vijay's staying with Mom and Shreya. Lakshmi lives here, she can take care of herself. Let's go. Now!"

I had never heard Dad use that tone of voice before. Slightly stunned, I let him pull me down the alleyway, toward the car. When we got to the *basti* entrance, the silver Range Rover was gone.

"Will Mom be okay?"

We were sitting in the parked car, waiting for Mom and Vijay to return.

"Of course, sweetheart," Dad said. He smiled at me reassuringly. "Shreya's a pro at handling these situations. And Mom's been in tighter spots than this one."

"Like what?" I said. I needed specifics.

"Hmm . . . ," Dad said. "Like remember when you made us go to the Toys "R" Us in Times Square on Christmas Eve?"

"Dad!" I complained, but I couldn't help smiling.

We heard a tap on the window. Dad unlocked the doors and Vijay and Mom piled into the front. They were both breathing heavily, like they had been running. Vijay slipped the baseball bat under the passenger seat and started the car quickly. He pulled us into the flowing traffic.

"Well, that was interesting!" Mom said. She leaned back against the headrest. Her eyes were shining. Sweat was running down her neck.

"What happened?" I said. "Where's Shreya? Is Lakshmi okay?"

Mom turned her head to look back at me. "Yes, sweetheart," she said. "Lakshmi and her dad are fine. Shreya's staying to clear a few things up. She'll meet us at the house."

I gave her my one-eyebrow raise—except this time it wasn't an act.

"Really, honey. Everything's fine."

"How'd you do it, Mom?" Anna said.

Mom let out a little laugh. "Let's just say it was lucky timing that I met with the housing minister yesterday. I gave him a call. He's already gotten rid of those two buffoons."

"But what about Lakshmi's house?"

"Not to worry," Mom said. "Shreya will get me some quotes. I'll type up our little scoop and email it to the minister. By morning, the whole *basti* will be safe."

She looked at our worried faces.

"If it makes you feel better, I can start right now."

We nodded.

Mom pulled her BlackBerry out of her handbag and began typing as she spoke:

"If there is any doubt about corruption at the highest levels of the Indian government, consider the case of an innocent young schoolgirl and the real estate titan who used his political connections to threaten her humble home—"

"Mom?" I said.

Dad silenced me by holding a finger up to his lips. "Let her write for a minute, Chloe," he said.

And so I did.

Chapter 26

We were sitting at the breakfast table on Sunday morning when the doorbell rang.

"*Now* who can it be," Mom grumbled. She was trying to read the newspaper.

"Probably just a shoeshine kid," Dad said. Ever since he had overtipped a shoeshine kid a few weeks ago, skinny boys with hopeful smiles and wooden shoeshine boxes slung over their shoulders rang our doorbell often, looking for work. Every inch of leather in our house was gleaming.

Dad plucked Lucy from her high chair, where she had been happily mashing bananas into her hair. Sundays are Dechen's day off, so that's when the wheels tend to fall off the bus. Our dining room table looked like a bomb had gone off. Dad tripped over one of my roller skates on the way to the front door. "Damn it, Chloe. . . ."

Then his voice changed. "Lakshmi!"

Anna and I sprang from the table and sprinted to the door. There were Lakshmi and her dad, smiling nervously in the doorway. I gave Lakshmi a big hug. Her dad touched his palms together and bowed his head in *namaste.*

"Please, please come in," Dad said, stepping aside to let them into the house.

"No." Lakshmi was shaking her head. "You come." She beckoned for us to follow her down the stairs. "We have some gift for you."

"Helen!" Dad called out to Mom. "Come see!"

Parked in front of our gate was an old wooden wagon attached to a rusty bicycle. The wagon was like a garden on wheels; it was brimming over with plants. There were thorny cacti and a squat aloe vera. There was a massive palm, its bulbous trunk stuck into a wooden crate. There was a slender ficus tree and a gnarled little bonsai. There was bamboo. But best of all was a large potted champa tree in the middle.

Lakshmi and I climbed up into the wagon, and that's when I noticed the champa was covered in tiny paper cranes. They were tied to the branches by sewing thread. There had to be dozens of them, maybe more.

"I make them from old paper, old magazine." Lakshmi shrugged as if to apologize.

"They're amazing! They're so tiny! How did you do it, Lakshmi?"

Lakshmi shrugged again, grinning.

Her dad was standing by the handlebars. "For you, madam," he said to my mom. He placed his right palm over his heart and bowed his head.

For once, Mom was speechless. "Thank you," she finally said. "I mean, it wasn't me. It was the girls. And my friend Shreya . . . But thank you. Thank you so very much."

It took us a while to get all the plants into the house. We carried them up pot by pot and lined them up along the edge of the balcony. It was hot out there, so Dad cranked the awning to give them some shade.

"I take it he doesn't know about your brown thumb?" I heard him whisper to Mom.

"Shhh!" she said, slapping him lightly on the arm.

Lakshmi and I were squatting by the champa tree, untangling the cranes that had gotten caught during the move.

"May I offer you some tea?" Mom said to Lakshmi's dad. He looked at her blankly.

"Chai, *Tantai*?" Lakshmi said.

Lakshmi's dad looked uncertain.

"Yes, please, Auntie," Lakshmi said for him.

While Mom went to the kitchen, Dad brought a couple of extra chairs out onto the balcony. Lakshmi's dad perched on the edge of one, his fingers fiddling with the hem of his kurta. He reminded me of Lakshmi on that first day in the park when she was so reluctant to come into our house. I practically had to drag her up the stairs.

How many things had changed since then.

When I first met Lakshmi, I assumed that she was a misfit and that she hated it—hated being different, hated being left out. Because that's how I felt. But the truth is, Lakshmi didn't care about that stuff. She didn't care what Anvi and Prisha thought. She didn't care about the other kids. Or even Ms. Puri.

Now it occurred to me: that's what I loved most about Lakshmi. That's why I felt happy when I was around her. Because she wasn't trying to be something different. She was always unapologetically herself.

You know the periodic table in chemistry? All those elements that you can combine to make different compounds but that you can never break down? O is always oxygen. He is always helium. They are what they are. They'll never change. That's what Lakshmi was like to me: perfect in her own form.

I thought of that moment I first saw her in school with her shiny black eyes sparkling mischievously and her knobby knees, how she had whistled out the window to Kali, her fingers stuck in the corners of her mouth. I thought of her stomping on Anvi's invitation and dancing in my room, arms flung over her head, eyes closed.

I was always trying so hard to fit in. But Lakshmi? She was just Lakshmi.

"My father, his English no good," Lakshmi was saying, shrugging at my dad.

"Well, it sure as hell beats my Hindi!" Dad replied cheerfully.

There was an awkward pause.

"Dad," Anna said, "people don't really swear much in India."

"Oh, right," Dad said. "Sorry."

When he tried to change topics, things only got worse. "Your wife?" he said to Lakshmi's dad. "Is she also, um, into gardening?"

I held my breath; I hadn't told anyone about Lakshmi's family.

A flash of pain crossed Lakshmi's father's face.

"My mother," Lakshmi jumped in. "She is not living."

Mom appeared with a tray of cookies and tea fixings and we all made ourselves busy, helping her transfer everything onto the table.

Lakshmi's dad took a sip of Mom's chai and struggled not to make a face. He reached for the sugar bowl and scooped five heaping teaspoons into his tea and then stirred it vigorously, the spoon clanking against the rim of the cup. When he pointed to the sky, I was sure it was a ploy to distract us so that he could dump his tea into one of the potted plants without anyone noticing. But then I followed his finger and saw the clouds rolling in, huge black puffs speeding across the sky.

"Rain!" Lakshmi yelped. She jumped up from her chair and pointed, too. "Chloe! Anna! Rain is coming!"

The wind had started to blow. Then thunder clapped.

"Come! Come!" Lakshmi yelled, grabbing me by the hand. We ran down the stairs, across the street, and into the park, kicking our shoes off onto the grass just as the first fat raindrops began to fall.

I have never felt rain like that. It pounded down so hard that it jumped back up from the ground, hitting us in both directions. Within seconds we were soaked. My T-shirt stuck to my chest like glue. The noise was deafening. It was so loud, I thought, *This is what it must feel like to stand inside a drum.*

We couldn't talk to each other because we couldn't hear. There was nothing to do but dance. And so we did. We lifted up our arms and we spun through the rain. We danced and danced—Lakshmi and me and Anna, too. Kali showed up, barking at the excitement.

"We do our dance!" Lakshmi yelled at me.

"What?"

"Our dance!" She cupped her hands around her mouth like a megaphone. "Annual . . . Day . . . dance!"

I nodded, and so we started from the beginning of our routine, slipping and sliding on the wet grass. When we got to the spins, my feet shot out from under me and I landed—*splat*—on my bum in the mud. Lakshmi was still spinning, so I picked up a great gob of mud and threw it at her. I missed, but it distracted her and she lost her balance and fell down next to me. Then we were laughing and laughing, bums in the mud, rain running down our faces. We pulled Anna down with us too.

Kali was prancing around, barking. She gripped the hem of Lakshmi's kurta in her teeth and tried to pull Lakshmi up. But that only made Lakshmi shriek louder.

Lakshmi threw a mud ball at Kali, hitting her on the snout, and Kali let go of the kurta. She shook her head to clean off the wet mud, then barked at Lakshmi, annoyed.

"Chloe? Anna?"

Mom was leaning over the edge of the balcony, peering out at us through the rain.

I waved at her, trying to show her that everything was all right, that we were just goofing around with the dog.

I saw Mom hesitate. She was going to yell something else—probably order us to shoo Kali away and come back inside, get cleaned up—but then she stopped herself. She smiled and waved back instead.

The rain was slowing. Exhausted, we plopped down in a circle under the champa tree, leaning back against its rough trunk, our hearts still beating fast. I closed my eyes and turned my face up, feeling the raindrops that filtered through the tree's thick leaves. They fell on my eyelids and my cheeks. When I opened my eyes, squinting up through the rain, I was under a bright green tree tent.

Just like Boston, I thought. *But then, different in almost every way.*

We stayed under our tree for a while, watching as the sky brightened over the park like night turning into day.

"I'm sorry, Lakshmi," I said. "About what happened in the bathroom at school. It was so stupid. And I was wrong. I was stupid and wrong."

There. Finally, I had said it. Finally, I had apologized.

Lakshmi didn't reply, but she reached over with one thin, rough hand and gave mine a short, tight squeeze. I reached over to pass the squeeze on to Anna. She didn't pull her hand away.

We were all quiet for a while. In fact, all of Delhi seemed

quiet. People had vanished from the streets. No cars passed. It was like a wet sponge had pressed down on the city, muffling the usual chaos.

"About what our dad said." It was Anna who broke the silence this time. "About your mom . . ."

Laskhmi pulled her knees up to her chin and hugged them. "She use Pond's cold cream," she said. "Every morning, she brush her hair—her hair black like night—and do my *choti*." Lakshmi ran both hands down her long braids, as if remembering.

We sat there for a few more minutes, watching the raindrops drip from the champa leaves.

Then Lakshmi poked me hard in the ribs. "You lucky, Chloe. You have two sister. You have *full* family."

I glanced over at Anna. Her eyes were closed, her head leaning back against the trunk of the tree. She must have felt my gaze, though, because she half smiled, her eyes still shut.

We were quiet for a few more minutes. Then Lakshmi poked me again. "I finish all the crane for you. Now you make your wish?" she said. "Your thousand-crane wish?"

I peeked out from under our green tree tent. Up on the balcony, Mom and Dad were still sipping Mom's awful chai and trying to chat with Lakshmi's dad despite the gulf between their languages. Lucy had stuck one bare foot out from under the awning and was trying to catch raindrops on her toes. A family of parrots squawked at her.

Now everything looked so much clearer to me. It was like the storm had power washed the city, clearing away all the summer heat and dust.

Lakshmi was right. I *was* lucky to have a full family, as loud and messy and American as it was.

I was still blond. And I still couldn't speak Hindi to save my life. But I had a new home that finally felt like home, even if it wasn't Boston. And I had a friend, a *real* friend— one who liked to climb trees and do origami and play in the rain, just like me.

"You take the wish, Lakshmi," I said. "You made the cranes. Besides, I don't need it anymore."

Nothing had changed and everything had changed.

Maybe I was still a misfit, but I was happy.

Acknowledgments

While some people, places, and incidents were inspired by real life, this book is a work of fiction, plain and simple. There is no Premium Academy, no Saxena Enterprises, no Chloe, and no Lakshmi.

There is, however, a progressive and highly inclusive school in Delhi that my own (very real) daughters had the privilege of attending. I would like to thank the administration, teachers, and staff at the Vasant Valley School, New Delhi, for the wonderful job they do every single day. Special thanks to Rachna Grewal, librarian at Vasant Valley, for her support of this project.

I could not have written this book without the people who kept my house afloat while I typed, especially Dolma, Manju, Lakshmi, and Vikram. Thank you all for making Delhi an easier place to live.

I would also like to thank the friends who supported me during the writing of this book, in particular Roopika Saran and Janya Gambir, who read an early draft of the manuscript: you gave me my happy dance in the kitchen. Also Anu Anand for her general enthusiasm. And my sister, Margaret Darnton Blodgett, who read several drafts of the manuscript and gave me valuable advice from the front lines of fourth grade.

Anita Roy at Zubaan: What would I have done without you? You are an exceptional editor and cherished friend.

To my indefatigable agent, Laura Langlie, and the fabulous editor she found me at Delacorte Press, Krista Vitola: thank you both for your faith in Chloe and in me. Thanks also to the copyediting team: Alison Kolani, Colleen Fellingham, and the eagle-eyed Heather Lockwood Hughes.

A quick shout-out to Stephen King, not because I'm a horror fan, but because his brilliant memoir, *On Writing*, taught me much about the craft.

Cut to my mother, Susan Darnton, who must be the polar opposite of Stephen King in every way, except their shared love of precise and varied vocabulary. Thanks, Mom, for filling our home with secondhand Betsy-Tacys and for taking us kids to the Princeton Public Library. To Dudley Carlson, the children's librarian at that magical place: you cannot know how much you touched my life, mainly by leaning down and listening—and then plucking the perfect book from what seemed like miles of metal shelves. Thank you for your years of service to the Princeton community.

Thanks also to my teachers, especially the late Mr. Dougherty of the John Witherspoon Middle School in Princeton and Peter Osnos, founder and editor-at-large at PublicAffairs.

Lastly, I would like to thank the two most important men in my life: my father, Robert Darnton, who has always encouraged me to write, and my husband, Steve Stepanian, who came up with this zany Indian adventure in the first place—and then mixed the G&Ts to survive it.

To my three graces, Sophie, Charlotte, and Elizabeth: I love you.

Questions for Readers

In her email to Katie Standish, Chloe writes that Lakshmi isn't "really like the other girls at school" (p. 124). How is Lakshmi different? What about your classmates? Are they all the same? If not, what makes them different?

Over dinner, Chloe's dad mentions the Right to Education Act, which declares that education is a fundamental right of all children in India. (Please turn the page for more information on the RTE Act.) Do you think education should be a fundamental right, enforceable by law? Why or why not?

Due to the Right to Education Act, disadvantaged children like Lakshmi are being admitted in greater numbers to private schools throughout India. What do you think that's like for those children? How about for the teachers in those schools? Should schools do anything special to support disadvantaged children and their teachers? Why or why not?

At your school, is everyone invited to birthday parties? Does everybody go? Why or why not?

In the book, Chloe learns empathy, which is an understanding that other people have feelings and that those feelings matter. She puts herself in Lakshmi's shoes and sees the world from Lakshmi's perspective. She comes to realize that though people may come from very different backgrounds, they all have feelings and those feelings matter. Anvi does not feel empathy; she is mean to Lakshmi because she sees Lakshmi as different. Do you sometimes feel empathy? When? Do you think empathy makes people weaker or stronger?

In Delhi, there are an estimated five million people living in unauthorized settlements. They often face the threat of eviction. Do you think this is fair? What would it feel like to lose *your* home?

Chloe calls herself a misfit (pp. 201 and 207). Have you ever felt like a misfit? When and why? How did it make you feel?

The Right of Children to Free and Compulsory Education Act

In August 2009, the Parliament of India enacted a piece of legislation called the Right of Children to Free and Compulsory Education Act, or Right to Education Act (RTE). On April 1, 2010, when the RTE Act became law, India made education a fundamental, enforceable right. Here are some brief excerpts from that historic legislation:

> Every child of the age of six to fourteen years shall have a right to free and compulsory education in a neighborhood school till completion of elementary education.

> For the purposes of this Act a school . . . shall admit in class 1, to the extent of at least twenty-five percent of the strength of that class, children belonging to weaker section and disadvantaged group in the neighborhood and provide free and compulsory education till its completion.

> No child shall be liable to pay any kind of fee or charges or expenses, which may prevent him or her from pursuing and completing their elementary education.

No school or person shall, while admitting a child, collect any capitation fee and subject the child or his parents or guardian to any screening procedure.

No child shall be denied admission in a school for lack of age proof.

No child admitted in a school shall be held back in any class or expelled from school till the completion of elementary education.

No child shall be subjected to physical punishment or mental harassment.

Glossary

ayah: A domestic servant who typically works as a nanny/maid.

basti: An unauthorized settlement; a slum.

beta: Child; little one.

bindi: A dot or decoration worn on a woman's forehead, usually between her eyebrows.

chaat: Savory snacks, such as fried potatoes and chutney, usually sold at roadside stalls or food carts, also served at birthday parties and other festivities.

chai: Sweet and spicy tea boiled with milk.

"Chalo!": "Let's go!"

chapati: A flatbread similar to a tortilla.

chappals: Shoes, especially leather sandals.

charpoy: A simple bed made of ropes tied around a rough wooden frame with no mattress.

chhole: A spicy chickpea dish.

chhole bhature: Spicy chickpeas served with deep-fried bread.

chikki: Nut brittle, often made with peanuts and hot jaggery (cane sugar) syrup.

choti: Braids.

dal: Spiced lentils.

dehko: "Look!"

didi: "Sister"; an affectionate term for both sisters and ayahs (see above) or other helpers.

dosa: A Southern Indian–style crepe made from rice batter and lentils, often stuffed with potatoes and served with chutney and spicy sambar (see below).

dupatta: A long scarf, often worn as part of a *salwar kameez* (see below) to cover a woman's chest.

golgappa: A popular street snack; bit-sized, deep-fried shells, usually filled with potatoes, chickpeas, onions, and spiced tamarind juice.

goonda: A thug.

gulabi: Pink.

idli: Small, savory steamed lentil cakes, often eaten for breakfast with chutneys and *sambar* (see below).

jhuggi: An unauthorized settlement; a slum.

kajal: Kohl, eyeliner.

kati roll: A wrap sandwich, usually made of flatbread and stuffed with spicy chicken or vegetarian filling.

kurta: A tunic.

lahenga: A long skirt.

Lutyens: A British architect who, in the early twentieth century, designed the new colonial capital, bringing wide, tree-lined avenues and garden-ringed bungalows to New Delhi.

mirchi: Spicy.

naan: Flatbread baked in a tandoor oven.

namaste: A respectful greeting performed by pressing the palms together and bowing slightly; also a word often said aloud while doing the same.

paan: Betel leaf, usually stuffed with betel nut, lime, and spices and chewed as a stimulant; the juices are often spat out, leaving brown blotches on roads and sidewalks.

phool: Flower.

rajma chawall: Spiced red beans served with rice.

rupee: A unit of Indian currency, like the dollar.

salwar kameez: An outfit of loose, pajama-like trousers (*salwar*) with a tunic top (*kameez*).

sambar: A spicy, lentil-based stew, often served with *idlis* (see above) for breakfast, especially in South India.

tantai: "Father" in Tamil, a language spoken in Tamil Nadu, South India.

Tata Sky: Satellite television provider in India.

tiffin: Lunch box.

wallah: A generic term in Hindi meaning "the one." It usually refers to a person who provides a specific service; for example, the *phool* wallah, who sells flowers, or the *chai* wallah, who sells tea.

About the Author

Kate Darnton is a writer and book editor from Boston. She lived with her husband and three daughters in New Delhi for five years. They now live in Amsterdam.